The Urbana Free Library

To renew: call 217-367-4057
or go to "*urbanafreelibrary.org*"
and select "Renew/Request Items"

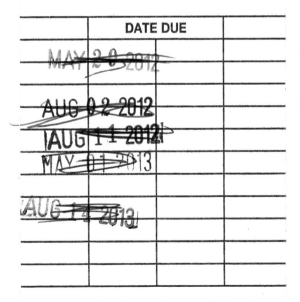

UNFORSAKEN

ALSO BY SOPHIE LITTLEFIELD

Banished

UNFORSAKEN

sophie Littlefield

Delacorte Press

Text copyright © 2011 by Sophie Littlefield
Jacket art copyright © 2011 by Robin Alfian
Jacket art retouching by Brian Sheridan

All rights reserved. Published in the United States by Delacorte Press, an imprint of Random House Children's Books, a division of Random House, Inc., New York.

Delacorte Press is a registered trademark and the colophon is a trademark of Random House, Inc.

Visit us on the Web! www.randomhouse.com/teens

Educators and librarians, for a variety of teaching tools, visit us at www.randomhouse.com/teachers

Library of Congress Cataloging-in-Publication Data
Littlefield, Sophie.
Unforsaken / Sophie Littlefield. — 1st ed.
p.   cm.
Summary: Having learned that she has powers both to heal people and to create zombies, sixteen-year-old Hailey is trying to lead a fairly normal life with her brother and aunt in Milwaukee, but when she attempts to contact her boyfriend, she brings dangerous villains—both alive and undead—to her doorstep.
ISBN 978-0-385-73854-5 (hc) — ISBN 978-0-385-90736-1 (lib. bdg.) —
ISBN 978-0-375-89496-1 (ebook)
[1. Zombies—Fiction. 2. Healers—Fiction. 3. Supernatural—Fiction. 4. Aunts—Fiction.]
I. Title
PZ7.L7359Un 2011
[Fic]—dc22
2010052997

The text of this book is set in 12.5-point Adobe Garamond.
Book design by Stephanie Moss

Printed in the United States of America

10 9 8 7 6 5 4 3 2 1

First Edition

Random House Children's Books supports the First Amendment and celebrates the right to read.

For Bryan Lamb and Eric Lamb

ACKNOWLEDGMENTS

Some books come easier than others. This one was a joy. Two people made it better than I could have imagined: Barbara Poelle, my agent, who knew exactly what was missing in the first draft—and my editor, Stephanie Elliott, who took time out of a very exciting year to bring the book to life.

CHAPTER 1

"ELEVEN'S LIKE . . . THE NEW TEN," Jess said, cracking herself up and spitting Coke on Gojo's coffee table. It had a glass top that showed every mark—fingerprints, smudges of guacamole, and the crumbs from the chips, which were made of blue corn but tasted like every other chip I'd ever had.

Still, it was a first, and out of habit I said the words in my head. *Blue corn chips.* When I got home—which had better be soon—I'd write it in my journal. It would be number 62.

But that was for later. Right now I had to focus.

"That makes no sense," Charlotte said, licking salt off her fingers. She was sitting on the floor between Gojo's legs. He leaned back on the couch with a beer dangling loose in one hand, the fingers of the other playing with Charlotte's wavy red hair.

It was Gojo's fifth beer since we'd gotten here. I'd counted.

"No, you know, really," Jess said, managing to stop giggling only to start up again. I was pretty sure she didn't usually drink as much as she had tonight. Not like Charlotte, who drank more than Jess and me put together and you couldn't tell. "Eleven o'clock isn't as late now that we're going to be juniors. It's like the new *ten* o'clock. You know, like . . . black is the new . . . no, wait."

"Olive," I said. "Olive green, it's the new black. You know, neutral? I read it in *Vogue*."

I wasn't making it up; I really had read it in *Vogue* the day before when Prairie and I went for groceries. We went twice a week, pushing Chub in the shopping cart and buying all kinds of expensive gourmet stuff I'd never seen when I lived in Gypsum, Missouri. Now we lived in downtown Milwaukee, which wasn't exactly L.A. or New York, but our building had a concierge and our grocery store sold things like squid ink pasta and herbed chèvre and Italian grapefruit soda (numbers 34, 35 and 36).

We always bought a magazine at the store, and then I read the articles to Prairie while she cooked. She said I ought to do the cooking since she worked all day, and she was right, but I saw how much she enjoyed it, making things for the two of us. I tried to do my part by cleaning up, keeping the apartment neat and doing the laundry. And she never complained. None of us did, not even Chub, whose chores consisted mostly of helping set the table and picking up his toys at the end of the day.

We kept things light; we never argued. Two months after we burned the lab down, I think we were still kind of surprised we'd made it out alive—and I was still getting used to living with my aunt. Especially since until a few months ago I hadn't even known I had any living relatives besides Gram.

If it was weird how Prairie and I came to be in each other's lives, it was also really easy living together. I was comfortable with her, and I never had to think about what to say around her. Not like I did with Jess and Charlotte. It should have been a natural fit, since the three of us had so much in common: we were all sixteen, all starting our junior year at Grosbeck Academy in the fall, all interested in the same things—clothes, boys, music, makeup.

But I had a secret: they were the first real friends I'd ever had.

That was a secret I meant to keep. Which was why I was sitting here in an apartment across the tennis courts from ours, an apartment that belonged to a twenty-eight-year-old bank branch manager named Gordon Johnson, who drove a red BMW and had told us to call him Gojo and offered us Cokes a week ago Sunday, when Charlotte started talking to him at the pool late in the afternoon.

That day he'd invited us up to his place and given us sodas from the fridge, and we'd played blackjack. Today—another lazy Sunday afternoon that stretched into evening, all three of us calling home to say we were at each other's places, lies that weren't questioned by Charlotte's or Jess's mom—

Gojo had put frozen pizzas in the oven, scooped guacamole from a jar and poured our Cokes into tall glasses, then topped them off with whiskey.

It wasn't very good whiskey. In fact, it was dirt cheap. I knew that because my grandmother used to serve it to her customers, and if there was one thing you could say about Gram, it was that she'd been as cheap as they come.

I'd poured my drink out in the sink and filled my glass with straight-up Coke. That was at six o'clock, when we'd first arrived. I'd kept doing it all night, whenever Gojo topped our drinks off. But now it was nearly eleven, half an hour past when I'd said I'd be home, and I had a decision to make.

Should I leave and earn the derision of Jess and Charlotte, the first and only friends I'd ever made?

Or should I stay and give my aunt something to worry herself sick over?

A missed curfew didn't mean the same thing to me as it did to other kids. If I didn't come home when I'd said I would, Prairie would immediately think that *they* had found us.

And that we were as good as dead.

"Sorry, guys," I said, standing up and faking a yawn. "I'd love to stay, but I've got a driving lesson first thing tomorrow."

Jess gave me a forlorn little pout, but Charlotte fixed me with a chilly glare. "So sorry to hear it," she said coolly as Gojo ignored me and rubbed her neck, his fingers dipping into the back of her tank top. "See you at the pool."

"See you," I echoed, and by the time the door closed behind me, I could hear Jess giggling about something else, as though she'd already forgotten I'd been there.

"How's Charlotte and Jess?" Prairie asked after I'd given her my breathless apology for being late, making up a story about how we'd been watching a movie and lost track of time.

"Fine," I said, turning away from her and pouring myself a glass of water. I was a terrible liar, and I knew it.

I hadn't always been. Lying to Gram had been not only easy, but necessary. But with Prairie it was different. After all we'd been through, I felt bad lying to her.

At home, in the apartment where I spent nearly all my time, I let myself forget that she was now Holly Garrett and I was Amber Garrett. Prairie kept telling me that I needed to stop using our old names, that we were never going back. And I kept telling her I needed just a little more time. I knew from the way the line between her eyebrows deepened when I called her Prairie that she thought it was a mistake not to force the issue. But I also knew that Prairie had a hard time saying no to me.

I tried not to take advantage—except when it came to this one thing. I'd give up our old lives, our old names. Soon. Just not quite yet.

"Why don't you see if Jess and Charlotte want to go to the mall with us Tuesday?" Prairie continued, keeping her voice light. "I can get off a little early, we can try that new sushi place. My treat."

"Umm . . . sure. I'll ask them."

I tried to ignore the lump in my throat. Prairie was trying so hard—she knew how much it meant to me to fit in here. When we'd first moved to Milwaukee, there had been only a few weeks left in the school year, so she had made arrangements for me to attend a private high school in the fall, and I'd gotten an early start on the summer reading list. Prairie had been on the lookout for friends for me even then; she was so excited when school finally let out and I met Jess and Charlotte at the pool. In a couple of months I would be attending the exclusive Grosbeck Academy with Jess and Charlotte and four hundred girls just like them: pretty, spoiled girls who were used to getting everything they wanted.

Prairie made sure I had everything I needed to fit in. My closet was full of clothes from department stores and expensive boutiques. I had sandals in every color, to show off my pedicure. I had my own bathroom and enough cosmetics and hair products to fill all the cabinets. We had cable and high-speed Internet and great speakers.

No one could tell that three months ago I'd been a freak, an outcast, an orphan in thrift-store rags. A girl nobody wanted, least of all my drug-dealing grandmother, who was now buried in an unmarked grave, courtesy of the citizens of Gypsum.

"So it's a date, then," Prairie said, giving me a quick squeeze. She looked so pleased that I didn't say what I'd been trying to find words for: that maybe we could make it just the two of us. Just for a little longer.

I wanted—*needed*—to be accepted by Jess and Charlotte. Yet there was a part of me that wasn't ready. Not by a long shot.

CHAPTER 2

WHEN TUESDAY EVENING rolled around, I let Prairie down.

I waited until she got home to tell her. I told myself it was because she never took her phone into the lab where they conducted the experiments—she was part of a team doing some kind of research with high magnetic fields, and they couldn't take anything electronic into the lab with them—but the truth was that I could have left a message on her work phone, or her cell phone. I knew she checked both the minute she got out of the lab—after she checked the *other* phone, the one hidden in a pocket in the bottom of her purse.

I didn't call any of those numbers, though. At five, when Prairie came home all excited about our evening out, I was waiting for her, sitting on one of the barstools in the kitchen.

Her smile slipped a little when she saw what I was wearing. I knew the blue halter top showed too much, and the white shorts were too short—and the platform sandals were way over the top. But Charlotte had called after lunch, and once she'd talked me into her plan, she coached me about what to wear—"You'll look so hot, Amber"—and if I showed up in something else, it would be proof that I didn't fit in.

I crossed my arms over my chest. "I'm going out with Charlotte and Jess," I mumbled, not meeting Prairie's eyes.

"Oh, are they . . . We're not going for sushi?"

I shook my head and reached for my purse. In my sandals I was taller than Prairie. "Change of plans. We're going to catch a movie and then maybe go out for a late dinner, just me and them."

There was a pause, and I edged toward the door, feeling my face go hot.

"Okay. Just . . . call me if you're going to be late," Prairie said in a small voice, and hearing her try to stay cheerful was worse than her getting angry and yelling at me.

Maybe that was why I snapped at her. "I *always* call. Remember? I'm going to have to grow up eventually, Prairie. Or do you plan on keeping me in this—this *cage* for the rest of my life?"

Then I ran for the door and let it slam behind me, trying to drown out the shocked silence. But I couldn't put the image of Prairie out of my mind: she stood there in her neat tailored clothes with her hand to her throat, looking pretty and elegant and more worried than I'd ever seen her.

*　　*　　*

I might have said no to Charlotte, except that Gojo was bringing his summer interns. And they were nineteen and twenty, business students at the university, which made it seem almost okay. Well, at least a lot more okay than when it was just us and a twenty-eight-year-old guy.

We met at Charlotte's town house, on the other side of the development. She'd snuck a bottle of vodka into her room. She mixed it with raspberry Crystal Light in big plastic glasses. While we did each other's makeup, I drank some, instead of just pretending, like I usually did. It seemed to me that Charlotte was watching me more carefully than usual, like she was coming to a conclusion about me that would determine whether I would still be a part of the in crowd when summer ended.

Jess had told me that Charlotte was a big deal at Grosbeck. I didn't doubt it, and I also thought I knew why Charlotte had chosen Jess as her best friend: Jess was rich and pretty but she was neither smart nor opinionated. She did as she was told, and she seemed more than happy to let Charlotte make all the decisions.

Like now: Charlotte told her to try the green eyeliner under her lower lashes, and Jess just sat there like one of those makeup Barbie heads I'd always wanted when I was a little girl, letting Charlotte draw it on. When Charlotte turned to me, I snapped shut the compact I was holding before she could start in on me, and announced that I was ready. I could see that Charlotte had something on the tip of her tongue, but with my short platinum hair and the clothes I was wearing, too much eye makeup would make me look like a slut, which was *not* how I wanted to look in front of a bunch of strangers.

In fact, I almost went home after we said goodbye to Charlotte's folks. I thought we were going to try to sneak out, but Charlotte took us straight past her mom and stepdad, who were watching TV in the family room. Charlotte's mom jumped up, spilling her wine, and told us to have fun at the movie. She gave Charlotte a noisy peck on the cheek and then squinted at me and Jess, swaying slightly on her spike heels.

"Don't you girls look sweet?" she said, breathing wine in my face and giving me a view of her ample cleavage, which her tight pink top didn't cover very well.

At least I knew where Charlotte got her sense of style.

By the time we'd walked to Gojo's apartment, my sandals were hurting my feet. Outside his door, Charlotte gave us a quick once-over, tugging at Jess's top, then fluffing the front of my hair so it swooped over one eye, which made it hard to see. I pushed it back behind my ear. "Whatever," Charlotte sighed as Gojo opened the door, wearing a sunburn and a loud print shirt.

His interns, Justin and Calvin, didn't seem all that impressive to me. Justin was thin, with a red line of acne along his hairline, and Calvin had on a work shirt buttoned too high and jeans that looked like he'd ironed them. They didn't match my image of the kind of guys Charlotte and Jess would hang out with, but maybe it was enough that they were older and eager to party with us. They'd already been drinking, it was clear. I decided to stick to water for the rest of the night, since I was already feeling the vodka. Until I met Charlotte, I'd had alcohol only once, back when I lived with Gram. I tasted one of her beers when I was ten and trying to figure out why she liked it so much.

By nine-thirty we still hadn't had dinner—Gojo had promised to get takeout but had somehow never gotten around to it—and the party had splintered into couples. Gojo turned the lights down low before he and Charlotte went out on the balcony, leaving the door open, so we could hear them murmuring and laughing. Justin pulled Jess down on his lap on the couch and she pretended to resist, but it was pretty clear where they were headed, especially since she was probably the drunkest person there. She'd been pounding rum-and-Cokes since we'd arrived.

Calvin seemed just about as thrilled to be stuck with me as I was to be with him. I'd been making small talk, asking him about school, what he was studying—he wanted to go back to his hometown and open a mobile computer-repair franchise—and he'd been pushing his beer bottle in circles on the table, not looking at me.

"I'm, uh, only sixteen," I blurted after an awkward lull in the conversation. That made his eyes go wide and I knew my suspicion was correct: Gojo had told them we were older.

"I'm only here because Johnson made it sound like it would come up in my performance review if I didn't show up," Calvin admitted. "He's always making us go to happy hour."

"You don't want to?" I asked, surprised. "I mean . . ."

"I've got a girlfriend," Calvin said, blushing. "A pretty serious one."

After that, I didn't feel so bad about leaving. It helped to know that there was someone else who felt out of place, who didn't want to be there. Calvin said he'd walk me home, and I said he didn't have to, and he said he'd feel better about it, that you never knew after dark, and I had to suppress a smile, wondering what he'd think if he knew exactly how much trouble I'd actually gotten into in the last year.

"I'm going to head home," I said loudly, gathering up my things.

No response from the patio, which had been quiet for a while. But Jess staggered to her feet, almost tripping over Justin.

"No, don't go, Amber," she said, her words slurring. "It won't be—it won't be—"

I saw it coming, saw her teetering in slow motion, trying to get her balance, before she took a faltering step in her clunky flip-flops, twisted her ankle and went down.

She crashed onto the coffee table, and from the sounds of things breaking, I was sure that the glass top had shattered, but when I raced across the room, I saw that the noise had been made by the glasses and bottles that had accumulated there over the course of the night. Most had fallen to the carpeted floor, spilling their contents, but Jess had broken a couple of glasses, and as I helped her up from the mess, I saw blood dripping down her arm.

"Amber," she said, her lips bunched in a confused pout. "I think I cut myself."

That was when I noticed a two-inch piece of glass embedded in her wrist. And the blood wasn't just flowing from the wound—it was pumping out in rhythmic spurts.

"Holy shit," Justin said, backing away from the mess on the floor.

"That looks bad," Calvin said. "Why don't you take her into the bathroom, Amber, and we can clean up out here. Give me a sec, I'll be right there."

Jess leaned against me, staring at her arm in detached amazement. The bottom of her shirt was already soaked in blood. I heard Calvin and Gojo arguing on the patio, but I closed the bathroom door behind us.

In the light, it looked even worse. I helped Jess sit down on the edge of the tub, but she slid onto the tiled floor, leaning into the corner where the tub met the wall, her eyelids drifting down. I knew she was drunk, but was she already weak from losing so much blood? It looked like at least a cup had leaked from her wrist, and I suspected that if I pulled the shard out, the blood would flow even faster.

I felt my knees buckle, and my vision clouded. The murmur of the ancient voices swirled and crescendoed in my mind, blocking out everything else. My fingers twitched and my heartbeat slowed to a steady, echoing rhythm.

Calvin pushed open the bathroom door. "*Jesus*—you okay, Amber? You're not going to, like, faint or something, are you?"

"No, I . . . ," I managed to choke out, my throat dry, my hands shaking from the effort of trying not to touch Jess.

I couldn't do it. Not here. I couldn't let them know, couldn't let them see. I'd worked so hard to fit in since we'd come to Milwaukee. I was starting school in two short months, and I just wanted to be a normal girl in a normal high school with normal friends and normal habits.

And the thing I longed to do was not normal at all.

CHAPTER 3

I HEARD CALVIN draw his breath in sharply. "She needs an ambulance. *Fast.* Stay with her."

And he was gone.

I lowered myself to the floor next to Jess, holding on to the towel bar for support, but the desire to touch her grew so intense I had to jam my hands under my knees to stop myself.

"Amber," Jess said, her voice soft and dreamy. "You have such pretty eyes. They're like . . ."

Her voice faded as she looked down at her wrist. Her mouth made a sad little o and she slumped against the wall. "I think I'm going to sleep now," she said.

The blood flow hadn't slowed. The puddle under her was growing at an alarming rate. Outside I could hear Calvin yelling, and Gojo, too—something about his carpet—and I knew.

If I didn't do something quickly, Jess was going to die.

And just like that, I threw away all my plans, my dreams, my wishes. I wasn't going to be normal. I wasn't going to fit in. I wasn't going to have friends like other girls, or sleepovers, or homecoming dances, or cheerleading tryouts. I looked like a different girl from the one I used to be, with my expensive wardrobe and makeup and haircut, but on the inside, I was exactly the same: a freak.

If I waited too long, I would make things infinitely worse. I had made that mistake once before and sworn I would never make it again.

I couldn't let her die. I put my hands on Jess's wrist and carefully removed the glass shard, trying to ignore the blood that spurted out. She made a soft mewling sound, but I barely heard her as my fingers slipped on the slick warm blood and the words swirled faster, and my eyes drifted shut and the energy coiled and gathered and reversed its flow, out through my arms, through my fingertips and into Jess, as I whispered the ancient chant—

—and I felt her respond to my touch, the ragged torn skin skimming over, the blood flow slowing, the veins and tendons knitting back together. I continued to whisper until I felt her heartbeat, strong and steady, under my touch, and then I opened my eyes just as the bathroom door burst open.

"Johnson's called a . . . Jesus, Amber, what—"

I followed his gaze and saw what he was seeing: my legs, shorts, hands and forearms were covered in Jess's blood. Next to me, she yawned and ran a bloody hand through her hair, leaving red smears on her cheek and forehead.

"I thought I was going to lose it there for a minute," she said conversationally. "I just can't hold my liquor—*oh.*"

It was as though she was noticing the blood for the first time.

I reached for a hand towel.

"I, um, actually don't think it's that bad," I mumbled as I began to mop up the blood and Jess lifted her arm to stare at her wrist. I kept mopping, rinsing the towel in the sink and wringing it out over and over, as Jess and Calvin searched for the wound and found only a thin pink line, and I tried to destroy the evidence of what I'd done.

We were in trouble, as it turned out, but not the kind I'd worried about. Charlotte was out the door after one quick look in the bathroom. She seemed happy to leave us to deal with the problem, so I guessed that was my answer to whether she was a true friend. I was trying to sober Jess up and Gojo was swearing and cleaning up the living room and kitchen, Calvin and Justin helping him without a word, when the EMTs arrived.

I was sure they didn't believe Gojo's story—that he'd heard the sound of breaking glass on the pool deck when he'd been out for an evening walk, and that he'd only brought us back to his place to offer first aid. But the EMTs were so puzzled over the wound—or rather, the lack of a wound—on

Jess's wrist that they didn't spend much time interrogating Gojo.

As they examined Jess, looking for the source of the blood that covered our clothes and created a trail on the carpet, I felt a faint swell of pride. *I* had taken care of Jess when no one else could; *I* had made her well. But I had also risked the new life that Prairie and I had so carefully constructed, and broken my secret promise to myself never to use the gift again.

Prairie and Jess's parents arrived within moments of each other as the EMTs were preparing Jess for the trip to the hospital. Jess's parents weren't as concerned about their daughter's condition as they were about her reputation. Or rather, *their* reputation. Her father was a developer who hoped to run for office, and her mother was thin and overdressed and looked like she could freeze you with her stare.

"What were you doing in a place like *this*?" they demanded, as though the expensive apartment complex was a seedy motel.

"Does your niece make a habit of getting drunk in strange men's apartments?" they asked Prairie, conveniently ignoring the facts that I was sober and Jess couldn't track the EMT's finger as he moved it from side to side in front of her face.

"Perhaps the girls should take a break from each other," they huffed as we were leaving.

Prairie and I didn't say much on the walk home. I started

to apologize a few times, but I didn't know where to begin. It wasn't that I'd been drinking, or that I'd been in a stranger's apartment, or even that I'd lied to her.

It was that I'd been willing to gamble all of our safety for a chance to fit in. As I went to my room, murmuring a good night to Prairie and Chub, I wished I could take it all back.

But more than anything, I wished I had never found out I was a Healer.

CHAPTER 4

CHUB WOKE ME up the next morning after he climbed out of his new big-boy bed and padded down the hall to my room, dragging his stuffed red dog. He liked to snuggle with me before we started the day.

"Clifford can go to school today," he said, his voice unusually serious. I propped myself up on my elbow and blinked the sleep out of my eyes.

"Clifford can't go to school," I said gently. "He needs to stay here and take a nap at home. But there's lots to do at school, right? Lots of fun stuff?"

"I want Clifford to come today," he whispered, a sad pout taking over his sweet mouth.

And then he stared in front of him, his eyes going wide and shiny, and my heart skipped, because I had seen him do this before, and I knew what it meant.

"Bad farm," he whispered.

"What?" I leaned closer, grabbed his hands and held them, trying to make him look at me.

"I'm going to the bad farm," he repeated, a mixture of resignation and fear in his voice.

"Is the bad farm at school?" I asked, thinking of Play-Skool plastic horses, toy barns, skirmishes with playmates, time-outs in the corner. Chub had learned lots of new words lately, but it was still hard to understand him sometimes. "Was someone mean to you? Did you get in trouble? Did you have a time-out?"

"Trouble," he repeated sadly.

"I'll talk to Prairie," I said. "She can talk to the teacher. Okay? Prairie's going to make sure you don't get in trouble." I pulled him into my arms and held him close.

I didn't have any idea what the bad farm was, but I did know two things. First, Chub didn't like it. And second, if he said he was going there, then unless someone stepped in and did something, it was going to happen.

Because Chub was a Seer.

I had him dressed and sitting down with a waffle and juice by the time Prairie finished getting ready for work. It was our routine, one I took pleasure in. I had been Chub's only care-giver when we lived with Gram—she wouldn't so much as change a dirty diaper or give him a cracker—and even though he loved Prairie, it was still me he wanted when he was upset or tired or hurt. It didn't matter that he wasn't really my little brother—especially since now we had documents saying that he was. Charlie Garrett was his new name, but we still called him Chub.

I handed Prairie her cup of coffee when she came into the kitchen, dressed in a silk blouse and a black skirt, pearl earrings and plain high-heeled black pumps. Besides her earrings, the only jewelry she wore was her antique ruby-and-silver pendant. I had one just like it; it had belonged to my mother. The necklaces had been handed down from Prairie's and my mother's great-great-great-great-great-great-grandmother, the one who had come over from Ireland in the eighteen hundreds, the one who had brought with her the gift of healing.

"I'm sorry," I blurted before Prairie could say anything. "What I did was stupid and I didn't think and I know I endangered us all and—"

"It's okay, Amber," Prairie said. She never called me Hailey anymore; she said the only way we could make sure we didn't make mistakes in public was to use our new names all the time. But the name still stung, and I forgot what I was saying and stared into my own steaming coffee cup.

"Maybe we can try again . . . ," she went on, hesitantly. "You know, the sushi place. I can try to come home early tonight."

I felt tears well up in my eyes. She was always like this— so patient with me, so understanding. Sometimes I thought it made things worse. "Aren't you mad?"

She gave me a smile tinged with sadness. She was still as beautiful as the first time I'd seen her, but now she looked tired most of the time. I knew she wasn't sleeping very well. "How could I be mad? You helped that girl, maybe saved her life. That's what the gift is for. You can't turn your back on it—neither of us can."

That might have been true, but it seemed like I was the only one who had been forced to heal lately. Prairie had healed Chub when he'd been hit by a stray bullet the night Gram was killed, but that was before I understood what I could do. Since then, it had been me, always *me*, who'd healed, who'd laid on hands and said the ancient words.

If Prairie had made her peace with the gift, why wasn't *she* the one who was called to use it? It didn't seem fair. I was the one who was in high school, the one who was under constant scrutiny, the one who had to find a way to fit in. Prairie was in her element in the lab, doing the work she loved, and I doubted that any of the geeks she worked with would notice if she had to step out of the office now and then to help the occasional accident victim or whatever.

Now wasn't the time to worry about it, though. I topped off Prairie's coffee for the road, and she and Chub left for the day. I'd been so caught up in my apology that I'd forgotten to mention Chub's problem at school, and I hoped the teacher would bring it up herself. If not, I'd tell Prairie tonight when she and Chub got home. Still, after I kissed Chub goodbye and gave Prairie a hug, I felt guilty and restless and frustrated all at once.

*　　*　　*

But it was Wednesday, the best day of the week—because on Wednesdays, I got to talk to Kaz.

This was another thing I kept from Prairie. And though I felt guilty about it, I didn't feel guilty enough to stop. I guess Kaz felt the same way, because his mom didn't know about our calls either.

Kaz was my boyfriend. Sort of. His mom, Anna, and Prairie had been friends for years, since he was a baby. Anna and Kaz had helped us a few months earlier, taking us in when we were on the run, and standing by us as things got more and more dangerous.

Somewhere along the way, Kaz and I had become more than friends. When Prairie and Chub and I left Chicago, Prairie and Anna told me and Kaz that they were sorry that we wouldn't be able to stay in touch, but we had to leave *everything* behind, including everyone we had ever known. No one from our old lives could know where we were.

Kaz and I had obeyed part of the rule: I'd never told him where we'd moved, and he hadn't asked. For all he knew, we were living in California or in Canada or even at the North Pole. But before I left, we'd figured out a way to talk so no one would know.

I couldn't call him at home. We had learned to plan for the worst at all times—which meant we had to assume that his house was being watched, that the phone lines were tapped. We couldn't even use cell phones, because they could be tracked.

We could have used our emergency phones, the prepaid cell phones each of us—me, Prairie, Anna, and Kaz—carried with us, the ones that were to be used only if the unthinkable happened. But Prairie checked the phones once a week and replaced them once a month. If I used mine, she'd know.

So that was out.

But Kaz had a summer job at the public library branch near their house, and on Wednesday afternoons, his task was to prepare the new children's books to go into circulation. That meant he had to enter them into the system and cover them with special protective bindings. It usually took a couple of hours, and he worked in the office that belonged to one of the reference librarians, because she didn't come in on Wednesdays.

And every Wednesday, I called him on that phone.

It was a windowless office, and there was no way anyone could be monitoring incoming calls for the entire library. I used my own cell phone and made sure that when the bill came, I was the one who paid it. That was easy enough to get past Prairie once I convinced her that I was old enough to learn about personal finances. Gram had never used a bank, but kept her money locked in an old desk drawer in her bedroom. I had never even had a bank account, and Prairie was happy for me to take on the responsibility.

No one bothered Kaz on Wednesday afternoons. With the office door closed, no one even remembered he was there. We talked for only half an hour at a time—caution had become a habit for both of us—and we never, ever talked about the future, because we both knew that it would be a pointless conversation.

After Prairie left for work, I took a long, hot shower and blow-dried my hair. I tried to read a book for a while but I couldn't focus on the story. I dusted and vacuumed, and at noon I fixed myself a sandwich. Then all I had to do was watch the minutes crawl by until one-thirty.

Finally it was time. I took my phone and a glass of iced tea out onto the balcony, where I had a great view of the pool. By the time I dialed the number, I couldn't keep a smile off my face.

But when Kaz answered, it was clear something was very wrong. I heard a clatter and a sharp intake of breath, and when he spoke, I knew something terrible had happened.

"Hailey, *hang up*—they know!"

I was so shocked I couldn't answer for a second, my heart hammering. I gripped the phone tightly. "What, Kaz? What happened?"

"There was an exterminator here all week—no one thought to check—they've gotten to the phones—Hailey, I had to sneak in here and if they find me—"

"An exterminator?" I interrupted, trying to make sense of what he was saying. "But how would they—"

"Think about it, Hailey—think about what they do. If they believe I've talked to you, they will find a way to go through every single outgoing and incoming call, for every line in this whole building. I'm going to hang up now and—" His voice cracked. "And we can't talk anymore."

I knew he was right. If they'd found Kaz, they'd use him any way they could to get to me and Prairie. But I couldn't accept it, couldn't accept the thought of never hearing his voice again. Now that I'd lost Jess and Charlotte, Kaz was all I had left—the only person in the world who cared about me besides Prairie and Chub—and the idea that this was the last time we'd speak, this was *goodbye*—

"But how will I, how will *we*, I mean, they can't just . . ."

"I've got to *go*. Hailey. Don't you understand—we *have* to. There's no other choice."

There was a crash and then an unfamiliar voice, a man speaking in clipped tones without emotion.

"We found him. Room 421. Start trace—"

The phone smashed into the cradle as Kaz hung up.

He hadn't been quick enough—because I'd kept him on the phone.

Everything was wrong, and it was my fault.

CHAPTER 5

FOR SEVERAL LONG MOMENTS I didn't move. I disconnected and stared at my phone—just a few ounces of plastic and metal, and yet I had used it to destroy every bit of security, of safety, that Prairie and I had worked so hard to create, and to bring danger straight to Kaz.

If only I'd hung up when he told me to . . .

If only I'd hung up . . .

But even that might not have been enough. We had hoped that they would never find us. We had wanted to keep Anna and Kaz completely out of it. When Prairie and Chub and I had driven north from Chicago a month ago, we had hoped that they would be forgotten, that the people searching for us would never find the humble bungalow in the middle of Chicago where we'd once taken shelter.

But somehow they'd found Kaz. And they were smart

enough to know that Anna and Kaz would never admit to being in contact with us. So they'd followed Kaz instead. Followed him to his job, pretending to be exterminators, biding their time, guessing that eventually he would lead them to us. And they had been right.

"Stupid," I muttered.

And then I snapped out of my trance.

I raced into the apartment, phone clutched in my hand, and grabbed my purse. Then I left, not even bothering to lock up. As I ran down the hallway, I dialed Prairie; when I got to the elevator, her phone was ringing.

I was alone in the elevator, and I paced the tiny space. The two-floor descent felt like it took an eternity as I waited for Prairie to pick up. The phone rang four times before going to her voice mail; I heard the familiar greeting I'd reached many times before.

"This is Holly Garrett. I'm currently away from my desk. . . ."

Stupid, stupid. I dug my nails into the soft flesh of my palm, furious with myself. But beating myself up wasn't going to fix things. I'd gotten us into this mess, and now I had to find a way to get us out.

Taxis weren't hard to come by at our apartment building. The complex was built on a strip of land that once formed the barrier between downtown Milwaukee and the grand old mansions of the East Side, and despite what Jess's parents thought, many young, rich professionals and families called it home, and cabbies often cruised by looking for fares.

Today was no exception. A man in expensive sunglasses and the kind of golf shirt that nobody plays golf in took the first cab I spotted, barely pausing in the conversation he was having on his earpiece to open the door.

I got the next one.

I'd become pretty good at it, stepping into the street a couple of paces and raising my hand high, looking like I meant business. I'd found that you had to look like you expected them to stop or they drove right by. If you had told me six months earlier that I would ever hail a cab, I would have thought you were crazy. In the entire time I lived in Gypsum, the only cabs I saw were on TV.

I reeled off the address of Chub's preschool, which Prairie had made me memorize the minute she signed Chub up. The ride took only ten minutes, but it seemed endless. I had to resist urging the cabbie to go faster. When we pulled up in front of the school, I threw some bills onto the front seat and bolted out of the cab.

I'd come only once before, with Prairie, back when Chub had been the newest kid there, and this time I took a wrong turn before finding the desk separating the reception area from the classrooms and play spaces. I could hear children shouting happily, but I couldn't see any of them. A young woman with a long braid down her back came through a frosted glass door, pulling it shut behind her. She held a stack of construction paper in one hand, and when she noticed me waiting, she gave me a tired smile.

"Can I help you?"

"Yes, I'm, um, I'm here to pick up my little brother. Charlie Garrett?"

"Charlie? Is something wrong?"

"No, no, I just . . . my aunt wanted me to pick him up for her. Holly. Holly Garrett."

Now the young woman frowned. "Holly hasn't called in."

"That's right. She hasn't had a chance to. She's tied up at work. She said I should just come get him. I can show you my ID if you want." One of the benefits of paying for a fake ID was that even though I didn't have a driver's license yet, I had a state ID card and a social security card that were guaranteed to be one hundred percent indistinguishable from real ones.

"Please give me a second," the woman said, but I saw the change on her face, the way her eyes turned opaque and suspicious. She went to a computer at the reception desk and typed for a moment with a small frown on her face. When she looked up at me, the suspicion had deepened. "I'm sorry, but your aunt is the only person authorized to pick Charlie up."

"But I'm his *sister*," I protested, even though I wasn't, not really. "Please, you have to let me take him. Maybe you can call her at work—"

I hadn't been able to get her to pick up, though, and I knew that calling her would be pointless. The woman shook her head, and her hand hovered above the keyboard, as though she was trying to make a decision. "If you come in with your aunt, and she signs a release form—"

"But there's no time for that!" I said. "I have to—it's an

emergency—look, I met the other teacher. When Chub—I mean, when Charlie first came here. The blond one. Maybe you can go get her?"

"I'm sorry," the woman repeated, but now she didn't sound sorry at all. "Charlie is fine, and he will stay here until your aunt returns to pick him up. There are no exceptions to the release policy."

I stared at her for a moment, trying to think of some way to prove to her that I was safe, that I wasn't crazy. But anything I said would just make me sound insane.

Finally I turned and left. Arguing further wouldn't help. I would simply have to find Prairie first.

It was a four-block walk from the preschool to the building where Prairie worked, and while I jogged down the sidewalk, dodging pedestrians, I checked my watch and tried to figure out how fast they could get here. I figured half an hour to trace the call. Once they found my number registered to Holly Garrett, they'd have to search employment records, and even then there was no way they would be able to find out where Chub went to preschool. Was there?

On the other hand, they could just torture the information out of Kaz. I knew there was nothing they wouldn't try if they needed to.

I ran faster.

When I got to Prairie's building, I burst through the doors and the receptionist glanced up from her magazine, startled. I was already digging through my purse. I found my ID card and slapped it on the counter.

"I'm Amber Garrett," I said, trying to catch my breath. "I'm here to see Holly Garrett. She works in the High Magnetic Field laboratory on the second floor. It's really, really important."

The receptionist, a spindly woman with thin gray hair and a blouse that hung on her frail frame, peered over reading glasses at me.

"You can go on up there, if you want," she said. "They got their own security."

I ran past her, muttering a quick thanks. I hit the up button at the elevator bank, then saw a door marked "Exit" and took the stairs instead, two at a time. The stairwell echoed with my pounding feet. The door to the second floor stuck before I forced it open onto a carpeted hall.

There was a pair of glass doors with a small square plaque identifying what was inside as the G. Laurence High Magnetic Field Laboratory. But the doors were locked.

I pounded on them, bruising my knuckles. After a few moments, the door swung open—just as I noticed a doorbell set in the wall.

"What's going on?" demanded a tall white-haired man in a cheap sports shirt with sweat stains under the arms. "What do you want?"

"I'm here to see Pr—to see Holly Garrett. Is she here?"

He blinked at me, looking more confused than annoyed.

"Are you her niece?"

"Yes, but—"

"You look like the pictures. She has pictures of you and

your little brother all over her cube. We work together. I'm Don Borelli."

I was surprised that Prairie would take such a risk. She was always so careful, so cautious. But then I remembered that it wasn't supposed to be a risk anymore. We didn't have secrets, other than the big one: that we used to be completely different people.

I forced a smile. "Yep, that's me. Can you help me find her? I— It's about Charlie. He's sick and I need her to come with me to the preschool because they won't release him to me."

I added a little earnest concern to my smile. See? I tried to telegraph. I'm only worried, not crazy. *Help me find my aunt.*

"Oh, I'm sorry to hear that. I'm sure we can help you find her," the man said, holding the door wide for me. "So hard when the little ones are sick, isn't it?"

I nodded my agreement. Borelli didn't strike me as father material. But then again, what did I know? I'd only recently learned that my dad was a crazed killer.

Borelli led me through a maze of cubicles, stopping in front of one, which I knew instantly was Prairie's. It wasn't just the pictures of me and Chub—several were pinned to the cubicle walls, just as Borelli had said—it was the tailored black jacket hung neatly on a wooden hanger, the orderly stacks of papers, the expensive pen resting on the blotter.

"Well, she's not at her desk," Borelli said unnecessarily, and winked at me. I wanted to throttle him, but I resisted.

"Maybe she's in the lab?" I suggested, trying to keep the panic out of my voice. "Can we try there?"

"I suppose so. Seeing as it's a bit of an emergency."

But when we got to the long rectangular room and peered through the large windows at the enormous machines, there was no sign of Prairie. I felt the panic gaining strength and rising in my chest.

Two men walked by, laughing at some shared joke. Borelli stopped them.

"Hey, have you guys seen Holly? Her niece is looking for her."

They glanced at me with mild interest.

"Yeah, you just missed her," one of them said. "She went out to lunch with a couple of friends."

"Who?" I demanded.

"Two guys—you know, around her age."

"What were they wearing? What did they look like?" I asked.

"Uh, shirts, plain shirts—one of them had a jacket, black, maybe, or blue? Short hair. They had short hair."

"Did they look like cops?"

Borelli was staring at me, eyebrows raised. But I couldn't think of a better way to describe the men who'd tried to kidnap us the last time, the ones who'd broken into Gram's house and started shooting.

The men glanced at each other, then back at me.

"Yeah, I guess so," the second one said. "They could have been cops. Why, is Holly in trouble with the law?"

The way he said it, I knew he thought he was joking.

But Prairie was in way more trouble than he could imagine.

They had her. They *had* her, and it was all my fault. After several weeks had passed, we'd convinced ourselves they'd given up, but we should have known better.

Men like that never gave up. And when they couldn't get to us, they'd gone after Kaz instead.

And now—because of my slowness, because of my stupidity—they'd found us after all.

"Thank you," I whispered, my throat dry with terror. I walked away from the group of confused men who thought they had been working with a nice lady named Holly Garrett.

When I got to the lobby, I ran.

CHAPTER 6

I'D RUN HARD on the way to Prairie's building, but I ran twice as hard now, back the way I'd come, toward the preschool. When I was only halfway there, I heard the sirens.

When I got within a block, my lungs screamed from the effort and I had to stop, holding on to a tree trunk for support. I couldn't risk getting any closer anyway, not after what I had done.

Three police cars had been parked hastily in front of the building. A cop stood next to one, leaning on the open door and talking into his pager. Another cop stood in the door of the preschool, holding the arm of an agitated woman—the young woman I'd talked to. She was trying to break away from him, crying and pointing down the street in my direction.

I slipped behind the tree, heart thudding.

She was telling them about me, the crazy girl who had come in half an hour earlier. She was telling them that *I* had taken Chub.

If only she knew. If I could get Chub back, I'd walk right up to the cops with my hands up. They could throw me in jail and I'd go gladly if only I could save Chub.

If there was anything in the world I could trade for Chub's and Prairie's safety, I would give it.

But I had nothing. And now I had to save myself before I could help them.

I slipped back down the street, trying to blend into the early lunchtime crowd, groups of people out enjoying the sunshine. When a bus pulled to the curb in front of me, I got on and picked an empty seat near the back.

I slumped down in my seat and tried to be invisible, and as the bus pulled away from the curb, I closed my eyes and pretended that if I couldn't see anyone else, then they couldn't see me, either. It was a game from when I was a little girl, a time that seemed so far away it might as well have happened to somebody else.

The bus made its slow, exhaust-emitting way downtown, toward the heart of the city, where Prairie and I often went to shop or try new restaurants. I eventually opened my eyes, half expecting to find a gun pointed at my face. But there were only a dozen or so bored-looking passengers, staring at the ads that ringed the bus, or at the floor, or at folded newspapers.

No one was looking at me.

I was trying to calm down and figure out what to do next when my phone rang. Not my cell phone, but the *other* one, the one that had never rung before.

I scrambled to fold back the hidden pocket at the bottom of my purse, my shaking fingers making it difficult. I dropped the phone on the floor and it skittered forward under the seats, and a heavyset woman with a lined face picked it up and handed it to me with a look of distaste.

I was too anxious to thank her. I grabbed it and hit the answer key.

"Hello?"

"Hailey, it's me."

Kaz. "Where are you? Are you safe?"

"On my honor."

Relief washed over me. *On my honor* was our safety phrase, something Kaz's dad used to say to him long ago, before he left to fight in a war and never came back. When Anna and Prairie had given us the phones, we had all settled on the phrase as a way to communicate that we were safe and alone, that there was no one with a knife at our throat or a gun at our temple.

"Oh my God, Kaz." I wanted to let the story rush out— *They have Chub and Prairie and I'm on a bus and the cops are after me*—but I knew I had to be careful. I moved to the back of the bus, where there were no other passengers who might overhear, and then I forced myself to take a deep breath before I told him everything: how I'd seen Prairie's jacket on the hanger, as if she was going to be back any moment; how the cop cars had pulled up in front of the preschool; and how I had heard the children's laughter but I hadn't been able to see Chub.

"Where are you now?"

"I'm on a bus. A city bus. I took the first one that came. I don't think anyone saw me. It's . . . we just passed the U.S. Bank building."

"Hailey." Kaz's voice was gentle. "I don't even know what city you're in, remember?"

That was right—I had never told. "I'm in Milwaukee," I said, and with that one revelation, I knew that everything had changed. We were a team again, me and Kaz, with an impossible challenge ahead of us. But I had learned to focus on the first step, and then the one after that, and then the one after that. We had a chance if we just put one foot in front of the other.

In my heart I knew that it was a fantasy, that our odds were nearly impossible. But for the moment I chose to pretend. After we settled on a plan, I hung up and looked out at the streets of downtown Milwaukee, at all the people going about their business. Nice, ordinary folks who'd never had to discover a terrible secret that changed their lives forever.

I managed to keep the denial going for a while.

When the city bus came within a few blocks of the Amtrak station, I got off and bought a ticket and a sandwich and a magazine I didn't read, and waited in the station with all the other passengers until it was time to depart.

A year earlier I wouldn't have known how to buy a ticket, where to wait, what to eat. Every decision would have frightened me. I had never left Missouri, and I could count on one hand the number of times I'd left Gypsum. I had never shopped in a department store, had a real haircut, eaten in a nice restaurant, gone to a concert, or kissed a boy.

Now I'd done all those things, and more. Prairie had been there for me every step of the way. She knew when I was afraid and she always made time for me, whether it was to take me on my first visit to a real doctor, to teach me how to ride public transportation, or to help me balance my checkbook. She'd created our new lives with great care, making my safety her foremost concern. And she'd been right to worry, even as I chafed under her rules, even as I broke them, even as I resented her for loving me enough to keep me safe. She'd given me everything, and I'd thrown it away.

As the Chicago skyline came into view outside the train window, I picked out the Sears Tower, the Hancock building, all the landmarks I'd come to love in the brief time that Prairie and I had lived with Anna and Kaz, and wondered if I was a city girl now.

But deep down I knew that despite my new confidence, my new look, I still didn't know who or what I was.

I got off the train hoping Kaz would be waiting for me—and knowing that he wouldn't. We had learned to be a lot more careful than that. I kept my sunglasses on, an expensive pair that had been a recent splurge on a shopping trip with Prairie, and walked purposefully in the direction of the shops lining the edges of the train station. I pretended to window-shop, pausing in front of a little store jammed with racks of costume jewelry.

I lost track of how long I'd been standing there. A minute, two, five. I watched the reflection in the polished glass, a thousand people with a thousand different destinations.

"Hailey."

I had been waiting for his voice, but I still jumped; my thoughts fell away and I blinked and spun around and there he was, right in front of me, and for a moment I forgot everything else.

"Kaz," I managed to whisper, and then I was lost in his arms.

CHAPTER 7

"GIT UP," RATTLER SIKES muttered, his lips inches away from Derek Pollitt's freckled ear. It had been no problem letting himself in through a poorly secured ground-level window at Derek's place, which was really just the basement of his mother's crumbling ranch house on the west end of town, not far from the old Pack'n'Save they'd shut down when they built the Walmart Supercenter over in Casey. Kids took pot-shots at the sides of the Pack'n'Save building now, and spun donuts in the parking lot on days when slate skies left a slick layer of ice on the pavement.

Rattler himself had let out some of his extra energy there a few times on days when all that power inside him felt like it wanted to itch its way out and leave him twitching and empty, days when he felt like *it* controlled *him* rather than the other way around. He didn't like that feeling, no, not one bit.

Days like that he split wood for hours, working in the freezing cold with no shirt on, feeling the splinters bounce off his torso, smug in the knowledge that they'd leave no mark on him. Or he shot a couple dozen rounds at the *n* in the abandoned store's sign from across the parking lot, feeling the restlessness ease its way back down with every shot that met its mark.

Which was all of them.

Today, though, he hadn't come over to this side of town meaning to shoot anything. He'd shot enough yesterday. He'd seen them coming, waited stealthy and still in the corner of the parlor, and sure enough, in they came sneakin', too dumb to know what they were up against. Rattler nailed one of them in the heart and the other between the eyes, and weren't they a sight, tumbling to the floor like the cowards they were.

The thrill of the blood hunt was still in his fingers, making them sure and strong. And now he was about to sign himself up a lieutenant.

If that was what it was called, anyway. Rattler had never been in the service, didn't know anyone who'd served, and made the mental connection only because it sounded like a second-in-charge, a right-hand man, which was what he wanted. He didn't want a *partner*. He didn't need an *equal*. What Rattler wanted was someone who would do what he said without much fuss, someone who understood a basic concept and was clear on a result and would do what it took to get from one to the other without wanting to run the show.

And someone who was Banished. It might as well be another Banished. Not because Rattler needed anyone else's visions, especially given that there wasn't another man in the county who could predict which way the wind would blow to save his life, and hadn't been in an easy couple of generations, not since most everyone had gone and married outside and diluted the line. No. He wanted a Banished man because it felt right to him in the same way it felt right that he'd put on his grandpa's silver watch that didn't keep time and nodded as he left the house at the old family portrait of his great-grandparents that hung in his hall—because this was about getting back to the past, to the way it was meant to be, to the way it was ordained before the Families left the soil of that village in Ireland so many years ago.

Derek Pollitt wasn't the worst of them and he wasn't the best. He had a taste for weed and a pint-a-day rum habit, but that made him about ten times as reliable as the ones who'd gone down the prescription-drug road. Those ones twitched; those ones were about as skittish as a burnt cat. They forgot whether they were coming or going, and Rattler didn't need any of that.

Ironic, really, since he was doing this for *them*. For all the lame-ass diluted-blood breed of the Families, those who'd tossed away their heritage the first time they'd caught sight of a tight-fitting skirt, chasing tail all over the county and fathering any number of spawn with the gift so weak in their blood they'd be hard-pressed to know it was there. It didn't make any sense, since the Banished were drawn to each other—like bees to honey, the way a girl from the Families could set a man's heart to pounding—but a lot of men just went for the path of least resistance. The easy score. Then they got locked in, put a ring on a woman's finger and compounded their error by having more kids to taint the population with half-breeds. Hell, quarter-breeds, eighth-breeds, who knew? In fact, as far as Rattler was aware, there were only a few pure lines left—among them the Sikes and the Tarbells.

And it was Prairie Tarbell he aimed to bring back. He'd already fathered the girl Hailey with Prairie's sister, and no one could say it was his fault that Clover had hanged herself from a rafter before her baby took her first steps. Hell, he'd treated Clover Tarbell *good*—better than he had to, anyway. Rattler's mouth tightened in a stoic line as he thought about the other ones, the ones who'd resisted, the ones he'd had to raise a hand to.

Not in anger. He wasn't an angry man. An idealist, that was what he was—a visionary. Hell, they all ought to be thanking him. He was fine-looking; that was a fact. He'd fathered half a dozen fine-looking kids around town that he knew of, not counting the Tarbell girl, and every one of them had the strength of *his* blood in their veins, and since he only picked women with the strongest blood ties to their Banished ancestors, he was single-handedly turning around the ruination of the bloodline that Gypsum's once-proud citizens had allowed to happen.

Clover's girl was pureblood. *He* had done that. And when

he brought Prairie back, she'd give him children too. Hell, she wasn't much more than thirty; she had a decade of bearing left, easy—enough time to produce a damn brood.

It didn't even bother Rattler that they'd all be girls. He wasn't the kind of man who had to have a son, who wanted to teach a boy to toss a ball or skin a deer. Rattler wasn't father material and he didn't care. He was on this earth for one reason, the way he saw it, and that was to build the Banished line back up the way it was meant to be. And he was meant to do it with Prairie. It made him near upon insane that she couldn't see it, couldn't understand how it was meant to be between them—but he'd make her see. This time he'd *make* her see.

But first he had to get her back. And he couldn't do it alone. The failure in Chicago—his dead eye, which his daughter had stabbed before she and Prairie escaped, throbbed in fury at the thought—that failure filled him with shame and determination, but it also served him notice that Prairie and the girl had more backbone than he'd expected. More power.

The thought excited him even as it angered him.

"I said git up," Rattler said a bit louder, giving Derek's shoulder a good shove. Derek coughed, his breath foul with whiskey and cigarette smoke and rot.

"Wha . . . what? What do— Oh. Rattler." Derek put a hand to his face, squeezing the bridge of his nose with grimy fingers. He squinted and moaned faintly, then dragged himself up to a sitting position and raked his hands through his hair, body odor wafting from his undershirt as the bedclothes fell away. "What you want, anyhow?"

Rattler fingered the card in his pocket, the card he'd fished out of the wallet of one of the men who'd died in the ambush on his house. It had a name—*Prentiss*—and a phone number, written in blue ink. "Got a job."

Rattler saw Derek's jeans lying in a heap next to battered work boots on the floor. He picked them up and tossed them to Derek, letting the heavy metal buckle strike him in his soft gut.

"What kinda job?"

"The kind where you might could make some serious cash."

"How much?" Derek asked automatically as he kicked the sheets away so he could pull on his jeans.

"Five hunnert," Rattler said without thinking. It was what was left of the money he'd had in his pocket for most of a month, the money Mr. Chicago had given him for information. Too bad he hadn't held out for more; now Mr. Chicago was burnt up dead and a lot of that cash had gone to the doctor—he'd said he was a doctor, anyway—who had swabbed and cleaned and stitched Rattler's stabbed eye in a filthy South Side apartment.

Damn irony: Prairie could have fixed him faster, and for free.

Only this way, with his eye dead to the outside world, it seemed to have developed an inner life of its own. And Rattler wasn't sure but what it might be better like this.

He caught Derek staring while he pulled on a wadded-up work shirt. "That hurtin' you still?"

"No."

"Figure you can still drive an' all, with just the one eye?"

"Got here, didn't I?" Rattler put a little extra menace in his voice and that shut Derek up.

While he waited for Derek to piss and brush his teeth and gather up his guns, Rattler swiped a slingshot off a bookshelf, climbed the basement stairs and let himself out the front door of Mrs. Pollitt's house, ignoring her baleful glare as she lurked in a doorway in her flowery housedress. He picked rocks out of the gravel and winged them at a row of mailboxes across the drive. When a red bird swooped out from the branches of a tall oak, he remembered how his mama used to call them Mr. Robin Red Breast, even as his stone found its mark and the bird fell dead out of the sky without a sound and hit the ground in a burst of crimson feathers.

CHAPTER 8

"How did you get away?"

Kaz and I sat on a high-backed wooden bench that gave us a little privacy in the middle of all the early-evening commuters, and he put his arm around me and pulled me close. It felt so good to be with him again, his chin resting on my forehead, my face pressed against his neck as I inhaled his scent of soap and cotton.

He let me go reluctantly. "There wasn't a whole lot they could do. I mean, we were in Crystal's office, there were people passing by. . . . They, uh, had a gun on me at first, but honestly they seemed a lot more interested in the phone than in keeping me there."

"Yeah," I said bitterly. "Who knew exterminators were so good with technology? No one in the library thought that was a little strange?"

Kaz shrugged. "Even I didn't think anything about it. I mean, they were working up in the ceiling panels and down along the floorboards. They had the little sprayers and all. They even had people out of their offices for a few hours at a time so they could treat them."

"When they were really getting into the phones, setting up the trace or whatever."

"Yeah, I guess." He shook his head. "I just can't believe they'd do all that. I mean, that's a hell of a lot of planning, expense—"

"But it's the General, remember?"

We were both silent, thinking about that. We knew very little about the General, only that he was the mysterious ex-military figure Prairie had worked for in Chicago. Well, to be accurate, Prairie had worked for a man named Bryce Safian, and *Bryce* had worked for the General, a fact Prairie had accidentally learned from overheard conversations and files she was never meant to see.

Prairie and Bryce had already been keeping one secret: Prairie was a Healer, a member of an ancient clan called the Banished. Not all the Banished could heal, but they all had abilities that the rest of the world didn't. The men had visions of future events. Most Banished could recognize each other through an intuitive sense. And a very few of the women—including the women of the Tarbell family, like my mother and Prairie and my grandmother and her mother and *her* mother, all the way back to the Irish village where it all started—were Healers.

Bryce had thought Prairie was the only Healer still living in the United States. Then he found out about me. He decided to kidnap me and use me for research, but he didn't tell Prairie.

It wasn't the only thing he lied about. He'd led Prairie to believe she was helping to research ways of using her healing gift to reach larger populations of the injured and the ill, when really he was studying her, trying to figure out how to create Healers out of ordinary people.

But the General didn't care about healing people. He had discovered that if a Healer laid hands on a person right after the moment of death, the person lived on in an undead state for a while, his emotions and reasoning powers, his *soul*, gone. These people were able to follow directions, though, and the General meant to create and sell these "zombies" to foreign armies to be used in battle, as suicide bombers and mine clearers, to perform tasks that living soldiers could not be made to do. He also planned to use Banished men for their visions, selling their services to the military strategists. Attacking your enemies would be a hell of a lot easier if you had someone who could see their next move.

Foreign militaries, it turned out, would pay astonishing amounts of money for the General's zombies. Without Healers to create the zombies, he had nothing. So he came after me. But when Prairie found out, she located me first. She didn't know about Chub—she hadn't even known I existed—but she helped us escape and then we made our way to Chicago, where Kaz and his mom helped us burn down the lab with Bryce and all the zombies in it, so that no one would ever be able to create zombies again.

After that, when we went to Bryce's apartment to destroy his files, we discovered he had found another Healer. Three more, actually—Polish sisters descended from the Banished. Two of the sisters had died in the fire, and we sent the third back to Poland, where she would be safe.

A thought struck me. "Oh no," I gasped, "I forgot to call Zytka."

Zytka Walczak, the surviving sister, was the fifth person who carried an emergency phone. We hadn't seen her since we'd said our goodbyes at O'Hare two days after we burned down the lab.

"Try her now," Kaz urged.

I did, several times, but the phone rang and rang.

"Don't worry," Kaz said. "She's safe. They won't be able to find her in Poland."

I wasn't so sure, but we already had plenty to worry about.

"Chub saw something," I confessed, trying to keep my voice from breaking. "He was talking about a 'bad farm' this morning. I thought he was just, you know, talking about getting in trouble at school. If I'd just listened . . ."

"You couldn't know."

"Yes, but . . . if I'd just done what Prairie asked me to? I mean, I *lied* to her, Kaz. I swore to her I wasn't in touch with you."

Kaz sighed. "I lied too. To my mom, to Prairie. Hailey . . . even before you left, I knew there was no way I was going to let you go. I *never* intended to keep my promise."

That should have made it better, that I wasn't alone.

Instead I just felt more miserable. It was my fault we'd been found, my fault Chub and Prairie were gone.

"Listen, Hailey, I was seeing things too, only I didn't put it together." Kaz pounded the bench with a fist. "I just didn't figure it out."

"You . . . saw them coming?" I asked.

Kaz shook his head, clearly frustrated. "No. I mean, I've been having those same visions. You, and the wires. Guess we know what that was all about now."

Last week when we'd talked, he'd told me that he'd kept seeing me running, my hair flying, my legs moving so fast they were a blur. Neither of us had thought it meant danger. We joked that I ought to take up jogging. And the other thing . . . he'd said it was like a sped-up movie of a roller coaster on a track made of wire, a dizzying blaze of sparking energy flying by, a trip through a psychedelic grid that left him with a searing headache. I'd teased him, saying that he was spending too much time watching YouTube concert videos, but now I suspected he'd been seeing the trace itself, the moment the General's men pinpointed my location and everything fell apart.

"So they let you leave?"

Kaz shrugged. "They didn't stop me. I just walked out of the office. I knew they were focused on one thing, and that was tracing the call. I was afraid they might have someone posted at the entrance, but I just walked out into the street and kept going. I rode the el for a few hours, out to Blue Island, around the Loop a couple of times. By the time I came here, I was pretty sure no one had tried to come after me." His expression changed and he touched my cheek softly. "You're really okay?"

"Yes," I whispered, not trusting my voice. I closed my eyes and savored the feeling of safety for a moment.

Then I forced myself to pull away. "We need to get going. We can't stay here. . . ." I gestured at the lobby, with its soaring ceilings, the people hurrying to catch their trains. It wasn't a bad place to hide, but before long the evening commute would dwindle, and there would be no crowds to camouflage us.

Kaz nodded. "Yeah, we need to keep moving. I called Mom earlier. I told her that we would be gone for a while. That we had to find Prairie and Chub."

"Oh, Kaz," I said, dismayed, imagining Anna's reaction. She'd lost her husband in the first Gulf War, when Kaz was little, and had never remarried. Kaz was all she had.

"She didn't take it well," he said hoarsely, looking away for a moment.

"What if . . . if there's any chance the cops could get Chub and Prairie back—"

But Kaz cut me off. "Think about it, Hailey. If you're not . . . one of us? If you're just another person who's never had a vision and never healed anything and never heard of the Banished, if you're just doing your job and trying to catch bad guys and keep order, would you believe it? *Any* of it?"

I thought about how I'd resisted when Prairie first told

me what we were. How I'd refused to believe even after she'd proved it, after she'd healed a bullet wound in Chub's leg right before my eyes.

The mind refuses to believe what it knows is impossible.

Before I could answer Kaz, he took my hand again. The sensation—his touch, his warmth, the electric rightness of it—rocketed through me.

"Hailey, together we have a chance of finding Chub and Prairie. . . . Once we have them, we'll come straight back here and figure out what to do next. But for now it's down to us."

"What do you mean?"

"Me and you. We have to go get them. We're the strongest. We have my visions. You can keep us well. Mom will be safe here. She doesn't know anything, and the General must know that by now, since they've probably been watching the house and tapping our phone for weeks."

I looked in Kaz's pale gray eyes, saw his determination and energy. And I felt the current that ran between us, felt how it danced at the edge of my heart, in the Banished blood that ran through my veins, and I knew that when I was with him, my gift was stronger; *I* was stronger.

At that moment it felt strangely as though we were not alone. As though in addition to me and Kaz there was some presence, something larger than life and older than history and deeper than time, that reached to us across myth and impossibility and pushed us forward, that blessed and comforted and promised everything would be all right.

"Okay."

It was what Kaz had been waiting for, my permission, my agreement. But he hesitated a moment longer.

"They're all going to be all right."

I heard the fear in his voice and I knew he was saying that for himself as much as me. Leaving his mother behind was undoubtedly the hardest thing he'd ever done, but Kaz and I both knew that until we defeated the General once and for all, none of us would be safe. My shiny new life, the beautiful apartment and the new school and new friends, none of it had been real. We had all been waiting, knowing that this moment would come someday.

I'd seen the toll the last weeks had taken on Prairie, the worry on her face, the dark circles under her eyes. Maybe that was what parenting meant—constant fear of what might happen next. I didn't know. Gram had never acted like a parent to me. Neither Prairie nor I had ever really had a mother, and we'd never had fathers, either.

Only Kaz had grown up with someone who loved him more than life itself, and maybe that was what gave him the strength to leave now. Because he was protecting Anna. He was almost a man, or maybe he *was* a man, in the same way that some days I felt like I was an adult and others I missed being a child. But when I looked at Kaz, I saw it clearly: he would be strong for the ones who couldn't. For his mother, and Chub, and Prairie.

And I would be strong with him.

I put my hand in his. "I'm ready," I whispered.

We slipped out into the descending evening, the city easing into its night self around us, and I knew that whatever lay ahead of us, Kaz and I would give everything we had to make things right again.

Chapter 9

Prairie sat up straight in the upholstered chair and kept her expression impassive. They were watching her—she was sure of it—and they had been ever since they'd deposited her, still unconscious from whatever they'd given her, on the hotel bed. There was a beautiful sunset over Lake Michigan out her window. The room was on a high floor in what was clearly one of Chicago's finest hotels, but Prairie ignored the view. She would wait for them to make their next move, and she would not give them the satisfaction of seeing how afraid she was.

Whatever they'd given her must have taken many hours to wear off, because when she woke, curled up on the bed, the sun had already dipped low in the sky. She'd tried the phone and found it disconnected. The door was locked from the outside. She thought about pounding on the walls, but all that would accomplish was to bring them running, and that could easily make things worse.

Thoughts of Chub and Hailey made her almost desperate enough to take the chance, though. If the men had managed to find her, despite the new identities, despite how careful she had been, then all was lost. The General would have sent teams to the apartment, the preschool, everywhere at once, giving them no time to warn each other.

But Hailey was something special. She was smart and gifted and brave. And she had the blood running strong in her. She was the most powerful Healer Prairie had ever known, the hope and the future of the Banished.

Was it possible that Hailey could have escaped?

When the sun finally slipped under the horizon, leaving an orange glow on the water, the door opened and one of the men from the lab walked into the room. He was still wearing the black jacket he'd had on earlier, but he'd taken off his earpiece.

He looked around and nodded in approval. Prairie had smoothed the bedcovers neatly; the room looked undisturbed. She stood and faced him silently.

"We didn't have time for proper introductions," he said, extending a hand. He was about her age, handsome in a bland way. "I'm David Graybull. We'll be working together."

Prairie ignored his hand. *Working together.* Was he serious? "You dragged me out of my office at gunpoint. I'd say that's all the introduction I need."

Graybull's expression tightened, and he let his hand drop. "You don't need to make this harder on yourself," he said, but as he ushered her out of the room, he didn't try to make further conversation.

The hall was quiet and thickly carpeted. Graybull pulled a key ring from his pocket and worked at the locks of the next room down. Prairie looked up and down the hall and saw that it was oddly short, with only four doors and a single elevator. Prairie guessed they were on the penthouse floor, one that had been customized at what was no doubt a very high price.

"After you," Graybull said with an exaggerated sweep of his arm.

Inside, the drapes were drawn, and the room—twice the size of an ordinary hotel room—was dim. As Prairie's eyes adjusted, she saw several beds lined up along the wall and, on the opposite wall, two people working at computers, their faces illuminated by the monitors' glow. One of them was her other kidnapper, and one was a woman with a mass of curls around her face.

"Ah, Ms. Tarbell. Welcome. I'm Phil Cutler." The man rose from his computer.

"She's not feeling very friendly," Graybull said.

"Really." Cutler considered her for a moment. "Well, I suppose I might be a little . . . irritable myself. Maybe it will help to know that the boy is doing well. We just received a report from the lab. He had two chicken nuggets and some applesauce for dinner. Didn't think much of the Tater Tots, apparently."

"I want to see Chub," Prairie said quickly, trying to keep the desperation from her voice.

"All in good time," Cutler said. "Your niece, on the other hand, managed to . . . have other plans this afternoon. Most distressing."

Prairie bit down on her lip to keep from reacting. So it was true—they didn't have Hailey. Good girl, she thought, staring at a crack in the curtains, where the evening light filtered through.

"I'm sure you're hungry," Cutler continued. "We'll find you some dinner in a moment. We'll do everything we can to keep you comfortable here tonight, and tomorrow we'll get you acquainted with our setup."

"What setup?" Prairie demanded.

Cutler raised his eyebrow. "Oh, I think you can guess, Prairie. I understand you are a very resourceful woman. Still, our partnership will require your cooperation and . . . focus. Please. Take a look at our current subjects."

He gestured at the beds lining the other side of the room, and Prairie took a closer look. In the dimness, she hadn't noticed the banks of medical equipment at first, exam lighting and surgical spotlights focused here and there. Two of the three beds were occupied, the motionless figures covered with sheets up to the chin and connected to IV lines, feeding tubes, monitors—all kinds of life-sustaining measures.

Her heart plummeted as she realized what she was looking at: a crop of the dying, waiting to be "saved" by a Healer, given life without life.

The floor grew unsteady under her feet. Prairie knew this scene entirely too well. When she was sixteen, her high school boyfriend had been killed in a car accident—but she hadn't been strong enough to let him stay dead. Instead she had healed Vincent, healed him after death—the one thing that must never be done. She had turned him into the living dead, and he lingered on in the shadows, his body preserved by science in a setting not unlike this one. No one knew who he was, and no one cared; his body was the subject of endless research by scientists who could not understand how he lived on long after his flesh had withered.

She'd visited him, over and over, the pain fresh every time she stared into his unseeing eyes and touched the cold flesh of the arms that had once held her. For more than a decade, she'd snuck into the nursing home where he existed between life and death, his tissues pumped full of experimental chemicals. She pretended to be someone else. A volunteer. A church lady. Anyone but the girl who'd believed that she and Vincent would be together forever.

"These two came in over the weekend," Cutler continued, oblivious to her pain. "America's finest, gave their all for their country, blah blah blah. They haven't yet been . . . transitioned. That's where you come in."

Prairie couldn't keep a soft cry from escaping her lips.

Transitioned . . . such a bland word for the most horrific act she could imagine.

"No," she whispered. "No, I can't—I won't—"

"And when you're done, we'll send them on down to the lab, which you'll be happy to know we've set up in your old hometown. Great for the local economy and so forth."

"You've . . . you've got people in Gypsum?" Prairie's mind reeled at the thought. So many Banished concentrated in such a small place. They would be sitting ducks waiting to be picked off by the General, turned into lab rats, made to commit unthinkable acts.

"Oh hell yes. Got a real nice operation in the works. It would be better to fly these fellas straight there, but I guess you know how things work in the sticks. Can't get a decent bagel, much less a direct flight. So we bring in our . . . volunteers . . . by private car. These two will be heading down there next week, once you're done with them."

"I'll *never* help you."

"Oh, don't be hasty!" Cutler exclaimed, his voice taking on a hard edge. "There's someone here you'll want to talk to. Sharon, will you help her?"

Only then did Prairie realize that there was one more person in the room. In a far corner a wilted figure leaned in a chair, her face obscured by a bandage that circled her scalp, her arm in a sling. Her other wrist was manacled to the arm of the chair.

The woman working at the computers got up and went

to kneel next to the motionless woman, opening the manacles with a small key. When the woman didn't stir, Sharon took her good arm and guided her up, not without care. The woman stumbled to her feet and seemed to rouse herself from a stupor, then limped toward them with a look of bleak resignation on her bruised face.

Prairie searched her features, then took a step back in shock. "Zytka," she gasped. "How—"

Cutler chuckled. "Ah, I was *hoping* you'd be surprised. I suppose you've been disappointed that she's been out of touch. You see, there was a slight . . . problem with her flight to Poland. Irregularities with her documents, you might say. We were able to step in before the authorities got involved. Nasty business, deportation. Although I suppose they can't be careful enough these days, can they?"

As the pieces fell into place, Prairie's throat went dry. She remembered the silent tears that had streamed down Zytka's cheeks as she'd walked through security at O'Hare, planning to disappear among her countrymen, to build a new life and try to put the nightmare of her old one behind her.

"I realize that you probably thought you'd never see Zytka again," Cutler continued. "But after that unfortunate accident at the lab, we found ourselves understaffed. Luckily, we were able to persuade her to stay and help us rebuild."

"Do not do what he says," Zytka mumbled with effort, lifting a shaking hand to point at the beds lining the wall. Her voice was raw, and Prairie saw ugly purple bruises at her throat.

"What's wrong with her?" Prairie demanded. "What did you do to her?"

"Oh, *I* didn't do anything to her, personally," Cutler said. "And my colleagues only issued a, er, correction when she broke one of the very few rules we have here."

"What did she do?"

Cutler laughed, a chilling, soulless sound that echoed around the sterile room. "She decided to leave without telling anyone. She made it out the door—quite impressive really—but she was, er, *dissuaded* before she made it to the elevator, and as you can see, that was not a very comfortable experience."

Zytka took two tottering steps, one leg twisting as though it would buckle under her weight, and one of her arms hanging at a strange angle. She worked her jaw and spit at Cutler. It fell short, and Cutler looked at the saliva on the floor at his feet with distaste. "See to this, please."

He turned his back on the pathetic scene as Sharon gathered paper towels and a spray bottle of disinfectant while Graybull led Zytka gently but firmly back to her seat. Zytka pushed weakly at the man's hands, but she was no match for him.

"It's too bad, of course," Cutler said conversationally to Prairie as he took her arm and guided her toward the closest bed. "If she wasn't one of your own, you could fix her up far more quickly than we could."

Fix her up . . . heal her. So he knew that Healers were of no use to each other, a fact that had perplexed Bryce. It had been one of the things he was most looking forward to studying when he'd found out that Prairie had a niece. Back then, convinced that Bryce loved her and was working to combat disease, Prairie had told him almost everything—how the healing gift ran in Banished families, how Healers only bore girls, how the once-noble Seers had diluted their gift by marrying outside the Banished and become hateful and mean, addicted and lazy and stupid. How glad she was to have left Trashtown, and her childhood tormentors, behind.

Up close Prairie saw that the patient in the bed had nearly half a dozen tubes protruding from his body, including equipment for airway maintenance and cardioversion. He was receiving advanced life support. If the machines were disconnected, he would die within moments.

"I won't touch him," she vowed, clenching her hands tightly behind her. "I won't touch any of them."

"Oh, don't worry, we don't expect you to start work tonight," Cutler said, chuckling. "You've had a long day. You need your rest. I just couldn't wait to show you how much we've accomplished in such a short time. Impressive, no?"

Prairie shuddered. "This is . . . unconscionable."

Cutler tsked and pulled the sheet back from the body on the bed with a flourish. The young man's torso was swathed in bandages. Prairie reached involuntarily to touch the smooth, undamaged patch of exposed skin above the bandages. He was not yet even a man; he was a boy barely older than Kaz, shot down on foreign soil, far from home. She guessed that he'd lost a great deal of blood, that his brain had been deprived of oxygen long enough to leave his body unable to sustain life on its own.

"You want to touch him, don't you?" Cutler said, unable to restrain the excitement in his voice. "To heal him."

Prairie jerked her hand away and took a step back. "No! I told you, I won't do it."

"Oh, but I think you will," Cutler said. "In a few days, when you are settled in and ready to begin work, I will turn the machines off. This young man's heart will stop beating, and oxygen will cease to reach his brain. His systems will shut down. And then you will lay your hands on him and say those words. You'll do it because you cannot help yourself, deep inside. . . . Heal him, and we will leave your friends alone. Refuse, and we will be forced to go find Kazimierz and Anna Sawicki. Are you willing to gamble with their lives?"

"No," Prairie whispered. "Leave them alone!"

Cutler shrugged. "As you wish. And welcome to the team."

Chapter 10

Three or four blocks from the train station, Kaz's cell phone made the ting that signaled a text message. He dug it out of his pocket and glanced at the screen.

Then he frowned and showed it to me:

WE HAVE PRAIRIE TARBELL AND THE BOY

"They're . . . Oh God, Kaz."

"You think I should call them?"

"You have to," I said without hesitation. "Only we need to get rid of these. Wait."

I dug a pen out of my purse and wrote the number on my hand. Then I turned Kaz's phone off and threw it in a trash can. If these guys were good enough to track down Chub and Prairie that fast, Kaz's cell phone wouldn't give them any trouble. That they hadn't tracked him down yet was proof that they were only using him to get to me.

We caught the el and rode it north. Only after we'd cleared the city did we get out, at the Howard stop. A few blocks away was a tiny park, a triangle of mowed grass with concrete paths and a few scrubby shrubs. Already most of the benches had been claimed by homeless people: some beside carts loaded high with possessions, some lying on their sides asleep, faces obscured by caps and jackets slung like blankets over their still forms.

We found a bench that was unoccupied near the far edge, and I dug the emergency phone from my purse and handed it to Kaz. "They can't trace this one," I said, and then I turned my palm up so he could read the number I'd copied.

As he dialed, I leaned in close so that I could hear both sides of the conversation. The phone barely rang before it was picked up.

"Prentiss," a deep, clipped voice said.

"This is Kazimierz Sawicki." There was no hesitation or tremor in Kaz's voice. He sounded sure of himself, even dangerous. "I'd like to speak to the General."

I heard a dry chuckle. "'The General'? Only Safian ever called me that. Young man, it has been a long time since I wore the uniform of this country or any other. My name is simply Prentiss now. Alistair Prentiss."

"Where's Prairie and Chub?"

The man laughed again, a sound that held no trace of warmth. "So you want to get right to business, eh? No time to chat, to get to know one another?"

"All I need to know about you is that you have kidnapped two innocent people and I want them back."

I put my hand on Kaz's hard-muscled shoulder. He played lacrosse for St. Stephens High School in the city, and his training regimen had carved and strengthened his body. Despite my fear, despite the danger and uncertainty, I felt my fingers tighten against his skin, and my heart sped up to match the beat I sensed deep in his veins.

Prentiss laughed shortly. "I think there's a little more you need to understand, Kaz. Okay if I call you Kaz, isn't it? Since that's what your mother calls you."

I felt his muscles tense under my fingers, but when Kaz spoke again, his voice was cold and calm. "That's none of your business."

"Tell me, Kaz, you're doing very well in your AP bio class, aren't you?" Prentiss continued as though Kaz hadn't spoken. "I believe Mr. Tanenbaum was quite pleased with your lab report last week. I hope I'm not breaking any confidences when I tell you that you received a ninety-two on it. Enough to bring you up to a B-plus, if I'm not mistaken."

"How the hell do you know that?" Kaz demanded. "Tap into the Secret Service computers . . . *General?*"

I was learning something about Kaz: he didn't experience fear the way I did. He seemed to skip it and go directly to whatever emotion followed, to the thing I would feel in his circumstances only after I was finished feeling utterly terrified. In this case, it was anger, and I understood that, understood how violated it must make you feel to have someone finding out the most hidden details about your life.

But in my experience, anger had not served me well. It never paid to get angry at Gram; she'd just laugh her hard-voiced drunk laugh or yell obscenities at me. And it never changed things.

But Kaz was a warrior, like his father. Anna once told me that her husband, Tanek, had passed along a legacy of bravery and conviction—other Banished traits that had died out when the bloodline had been thinned beyond recognition.

"I already told you, my name is Alistair Prentiss. No title—my years in the official service of our great country are, regrettably, over. Now I must operate with, shall we say, sensitivity to the demands of national security."

"So, what, they threw you out of the army and now you've got some sort of grudge? Or is it all about money, selling to the highest bidder?"

Kaz knew as well as I did that if Safian had managed to use Healers to create and sell battle zombies, Prentiss stood to make a great deal of money. Unimaginable amounts.

"I shall pretend you did not say that," Prentiss snarled. "But I caution you, do not underestimate my convictions or my commitment. Do not make that mistake again."

"Yeah, whatever you say, Prentiss," Kaz muttered. "You're the great patriot, that what you're telling me?"

"Patriotism takes many forms, young man. I hired Safian because he was a pragmatist. You might call him a point-A-to-point-B thinker. And he was hungry. I used his hunger for money and affirmation—yes, I stroked his ego and encouraged him. It was easy."

"He's dead. Guess he wasn't the best choice after all."

"He was weak," Prentiss shot back. "Weak enough to fall for his subject, after we had set it up so perfectly. If you knew what lengths we went to, to maintain the illusion that your friend Prairie was working on those—those ridiculous holistic health practices—"

He spoke as though it pained him, as though the words themselves were foul. "That won't happen again. I learned, you see, from my mistakes. Putting one man in charge of the operation was too risky. Now there are several. Hand-selected, my young friend. And if it helps you make your peace with what you are about to do, allow me to reassure you that these . . . leaders, shall we call them, are most humane. They are not interested in hurting Prairie or Hailey. They will be grateful for the ladies' service, in fact, and accord them the dignity and respect of a fellow team member."

"Hailey's never going to be a member of your so-called team," Kaz said, his voice low and dangerous.

"Ah yes, we have your young romance to consider, don't we? How clumsy of me, to forget the illusions of puppy love, the way it makes tender hearts burst with noble thoughts. And hormones, unfortunately, which are a bit counter-productive."

Puppy love. To hear Prentiss mock my feelings for Kaz, his voice dripping with sarcasm as he used words neither of us had yet spoken aloud, drove a spike of hot fury into my mind. But that just cemented my determination: if I hadn't already been committed to fighting him, I would be now.

But Kaz refused to be sucked in. "You won't find Hailey. Ever."

"Really? Consider this, Kaz. If young Chub knew where she was, we would already know. Oh, don't worry, we wouldn't use anything so primitive as torture. We have other means. Let's just say that all our research into the machinations of the human mind has led to some very interesting discoveries. It would be accurate to say that none of the little boy's secrets are safe with us.

"So what happens when we find *you*, Kaz?" Prentiss went on in his oily voice. "If you know Hailey's whereabouts—and for the sake of argument, let's say that you find out somehow—how long do you think it will take us to get the information out of you?"

Kaz's gaze locked on mine, but he didn't blink.

"You won't find me."

"If you are foolish enough to take that gamble, and, young man, I am betting on you being as smart as your teachers think you are and realizing that the only course that makes sense is to cooperate with us, but if you wish to gamble with the little boy's safety, then let me assure you that you will also be jeopardizing your mother. Tell me, Kaz, would you like to know what she is doing now?"

Kaz was silent, lips parted, his grip on the phone so tight his knuckles showed white.

"She is staring out the kitchen window, no doubt wondering where you are. She is twisting that pretty brown hair around the fingers of her left hand. That is her habit, yes, when she is worried? And how worried she must be, about you." He knew exactly how to torment Kaz—and he was *enjoying* it. "I'll leave you with that thought, young Kazimierz," Prentiss said softly enough that I had to lean in close to hear. "When you decide to call me back—and you will, my friend, of that you can be sure—you may reach me at this number at any hour of the day. And now I must bid you good night."

I heard the click that signaled the end of the conversation, but Kaz stayed frozen with the phone to his ear.

"They're watching your mom," I whispered. "I'm so sorry."

"Yes, but they didn't follow us here," he said slowly. "And they don't know where we're going."

Where *were* we going? I thought of the money in my purse. A few twenties—how far would that take us? And then I thought of Prairie and was hit with a wave of guilt—not because she'd given me the money; I knew she wouldn't care about that. But because she was a prisoner now, unable to do anything but worry.

I could picture her thinking, chewing her lower lip, a habit we shared. I had put her in an impossible position. She was supposed to be taking care of me. She felt responsible.

But it was different for me. I was a kid. I wasn't responsible for anyone. And neither was Kaz.

That made it possible for us to risk everything to rescue her and Chub.

Kaz handed my phone back, but before I put it in my purse, I had a thought. Prairie had programmed all the emergency numbers. I wrote a quick text message to her, knowing that Prentiss would have had her searched, that her purse and the emergency phone had probably been taken from her first thing.

I LOVE YOU, I wrote. DON'T WORRY ABOUT US.

Then I hit Send, not caring who saw my message. Prentiss's men could intercept it; they could throw Prairie's phone away; they could lie to her. But they could never extinguish the feelings that had taken root in my cold, lonely heart.

CHAPTER 11

I LOVE YOU.

I had said those words to only one other person: Chub. When he came to live with us, he became my problem, as Gram couldn't be bothered to feed or change or bathe him. It took only a couple of days for me to know that he and I were linked forever, to learn the curve of his chubby cheeks and the way his little hands felt holding mine.

I didn't look at Kaz as I slipped the phone back into my pocket. He'd probably said it a hundred times. To his mother. Perhaps even his father, whom he'd known only a few short years.

And . . . I imagined him saying it to me. Could feel the words on my lips, could easily say it to him. But we had been strangers not long ago. And besides, we had a job to do.

"What now?" I asked.

"What do you think?"

I focused on his question. It was a welcome reprieve from my thoughts. "You could offer to trade me. We could set up a meeting place and—"

"No. Too dangerous. By the time we set up the exchange, it'd be too late. They've got all the advantages, Hailey. Technology, weapons, everything. They wouldn't give up anything and then they'd have you too."

"They don't have everything," I said softly. "They don't have you. They don't have Seers."

"We just need to think about what we're up against. Prentiss said he's got more people in charge now, Hailey. Not just one like before, when Bryce ran everything. I bet there's a lot more people than that at the new lab. More security, for one. And more staff, if they're trying to rebuild the research in the shortest possible time."

"I still think Prentiss must be ex-military," I said. It was the way he talked, as though he was used to being in command. "If he hires people like him, they wouldn't care where they work; they'd just move to the new facility, wherever Prentiss told them to go."

"Yeah," Kaz agreed grimly. "Prentiss probably has contacts everywhere. Contractors who work for governments all over the world, not just ours. Old buddies still on the inside, who are happy to take his calls, listen to his ideas, maybe have an inside track to approving projects or getting funding."

"And the Seers," I said. "If they could train people like

you, who could see what the enemy was doing, their movements, their strategies . . ."

"The visions don't work like that. I'm a strong Seer, a pureblood, and even I can't predict when they come or what they'll reveal."

"But Bryce was trying to develop ways around that, training Seers to control their visions."

What if Prentiss found a way to control someone as powerful as Kaz? It was terrifying to imagine Kaz's gift being manipulated by someone like Prentiss. I prayed that they hadn't figured out yet that Chub was a Seer. If they knew what Chub could do, they would never let him go.

"So," Kaz said, "us against the ex-military machine. They've got money, weapons, connections. We've got, uh . . ." He shrugged. "Well, we've got each other. No problem— ought to be a piece of cake."

He was trying to joke, but his voice was hollow. The park had emptied as the sky had grown dark. It was just us and the few homeless people who were making their home here for the night.

I shivered, partly from the chill of nightfall and partly from the fear in his voice. I touched Kaz's face, just a hesitant brush of my fingers against his cheek. I wanted to comfort him, and I moved without thinking.

But Kaz reacted by covering my hand with his and pressing it to his face. He took a shuddering breath and said my name, hardly more than a whisper.

"Hailey . . . I can't do this without you."

He couldn't do it without *me*. Kaz was strong and brave, and I was shocked by his admission. He circled his arms around me and I leaned against him and held on, and I could feel his heart beating through his shirt and his warm breath on my neck as he bent toward me, and his eyelashes brushed my forehead.

And then he kissed me and it was like the first time, the day we'd left Chicago, when we'd stolen a private moment in the shadow of his mother's garage.

It was like the first time but it was also different. That time had been about the newness of our relationship, innocent and tentative. That day had been a sweet little break from what had come before and what would come after, and it was almost like an illusion—we both knew it couldn't last but we were willing to pretend.

This kiss was something else. It started gently enough, like the first one had; Kaz brushed my lips with his. But then it changed.

The first time we'd kissed, Kaz's tongue had lightly caressed my lips and I had been surprised to discover I liked it. I'd thought about it a thousand times since. I'd wished I had been brave enough to take it further. I wanted a do-over; I wanted to kiss him forever.

And now it felt like that was what I was doing. From the second our lips met, it was like I was tasting him, only the more I tasted, the more I wanted, and things moved so fast and were so hot I couldn't keep track and I didn't want to. I didn't even know who started it—only that neither one of us was resisting. There was fear and danger in it—and also longing and need.

This is passion, was what I was thinking when we finally stopped. We opened our eyes, and I was embarrassed and about to look away when I saw the intensity in Kaz's expression. We were locked in a moment when time seemed to stop. We stayed that way for a long time—or maybe it only felt like a long time, maybe it was a half a second—and then we did it all again.

When Kaz finally pulled me against him with a low groan, I realized that it was night. I glanced down the path and saw a pair of middle-aged women watching us, their expressions amused, and I blushed. We were in public, in the middle of the city, and I had forgotten that, had forgotten everything, including—if only for a moment—Chub and Prairie.

I had practically forgotten my own name.

"Hailey," Kaz whispered, almost like he was reading my mind. "I'm glad you're here."

I nodded, not trusting myself to speak.

"It's cold," he said after a while, and gently pulled away from me. "Do you want my sweatshirt?"

I hadn't even noticed the cold until that moment, but it was true; my arms were covered with goose bumps. I started to say no, that I was fine, but Kaz unzipped his sweatshirt and held it for me while I put my arms into the sleeves and the sensation of his warmth wrapped around me.

"We've got to get going," he said gently.

"And we should probably get a good night's sleep," I said. "Before . . . we figure out what's next."

"Yeah. Uh. The thing is, we can't go back to my house."

"Well." I stared at a spot in the middle of his chest. He had on a Tar Heels lacrosse T-shirt and I focused on the twined *N* and *C*. "We could, um, there's motels, I guess. I mean, unless we want to find a shelter or something. I don't have much money, probably about sixty dollars."

"I've only got about thirty-five."

I did a quick calculation. The motels I'd stayed in with Prairie had cost close to a hundred dollars. And even if we did have enough, that wouldn't leave anything for food. Or a toothbrush. Or anything at all.

Unless . . .

"I do have a debit card." I rooted around in my backpack, came up with the designer wallet I'd talked Prairie into buying for me—right then I wished I had the cash she'd spent on it instead—and took out the cards that were part of my fake identity, the ones we had been planning to destroy, the ones I was now glad I'd kept. There was an ID card that identified me as a sophomore at Green Valley High, where I'd supposedly gone to school until my parents' tragic car accident. And then there was the debit card. It was set up so the money came out of Prairie's account—her fake account, registered to Holly Garrett.

Kaz knew of a motel not too far away. We started walking, holding hands like we were any other young couple on a date. The cracked sidewalk was littered with broken glass and trash. It wasn't a great neighborhood, I could tell, but people sat out on their porches, enjoying the spring night, and lights shone brightly inside little grocery stores and restaurants.

I remembered my first day in the city. It had been only a few months earlier but it felt like forever ago. I tried to remember a time when I hadn't known how the night sky looked when the stars competed with the lights from all the buildings. I tried to remember the sky over Gypsum, the way the stars looked almost like mist, there were so many of them.

I saw it clearly when I closed my eyes. I wasn't a Seer, like Kaz, and I didn't know what the next day would bring or how we were going to solve any of the problems we were facing. But when I shut my eyes, Kaz's hand warm around mine as we waited for the light to change so we could cross the busy street to the motel, the whole world sparkled.

CHAPTER 12

THE BED DIDN'T FEEL NICE.

Chub lay as quietly as he could and made himself small. The covers were scratchy and they smelled wrong. This was not like his new big-boy bed in the room next to Hailey's room. That bed was soft and the covers were fuzzy. And they were blue and there were airplanes with *propellers* and *wings*.

These were new words, words he could say now instead of just thinking them.

He could say words now because of Hailey. Before, words didn't come out right, but then a lot of things happened and Prairie came and Gram was gone and he and Hailey went to live with Prairie and now he could say words. He missed Hailey, but it was okay because she would come soon. Chub knew that for sure because he saw it in his mind-pictures.

And yesterday he saw a mind-picture of the tall man with

the beard and he was scared of the man, and he told Hailey but Hailey was making his waffle and she didn't hear him. But he should have told Hailey again. Because the jacket men came when he was at school and he was scared and one of the jacket men was talking to Miss Goode and the other one, the other one went sneak sneak sneak and then he picked him up and ran and his arm got twisty and there was shouting. Then push and shove and *ow*—get in the car, big glove hand on his face push hard fall on seat, and then nothing *no talking* something smelled funny and then he slept a long time and then he woke up and they went in the building and he had to go with the lady with the brown glasses and where was Prairie? And where was Hailey?

All day today the glasses lady had been trying to make him talk, but Chub knew about not talking and he was better at it than she was at making him talk, and he stayed quiet.

He could tell that made the lady with the brown glasses kind of mad. But she didn't do anything about it except try harder to play with him. But she wasn't very good at playing. She had square cards with pictures on them. Apple. Bell. Truck. On a table there was a hiding thing, and on the floor in a box were an apple and a bell and a truck and lots of other things. The lady with the brown glasses would take something out of the box and put it on the table, but it was behind the hiding thing so he couldn't see it. Then she would ask him which thing was on the table.

He didn't know. He couldn't see behind the hiding thing.

He could have told her that, but that would mean he would have to say words and today he wasn't saying words.

For lunch there was a sandwich but not like Hailey made them. Chips with bumps. Chub only liked plain chips. He drank his milk and ate his sandwich. He didn't want to make the lady mad. She didn't eat with him but she watched him eat. He wished she would stop watching him. He started to miss Hailey more and he almost let the words out but then he didn't. He wanted to go outside bad and almost told the lady but then he didn't. After lunch it was the table with the hiding thing again.

He got sleepy but the lady didn't know about taking a nap, so she didn't let him take a nap and he didn't tell her. At dinner he cried a little even though it was a good dinner, a hamburger with ketchup. The lady with the brown glasses came back with a man Chub hadn't seen before and that was scary. For a minute he thought maybe the lady was mad and brought the man to spank him but he didn't, he just asked Chub the same things the lady asked him, did he know where Hailey was, but Chub kept the words inside extra tight, he didn't know where she was but he was afraid the words would come out anyway, he kept them inside.

The lady with brown glasses gave him a new pair of pajamas, the ones from yesterday were gone, he didn't know where they were. Yesterday's pajamas had lions on them. Today's pajamas had stripes on them. He liked the lions and he liked the stripes but he did not like the way the pajamas smelled. Chub cried. But quiet, so the words couldn't get out, and then he went to bed and was very quiet and the brown-glasses lady left after a while.

But now he had woken up and there was a small light in the corner in the shape of a star, enough to see that there was no one in the room with him, just the bed and shelves and the desk with the hiding thing, but the lady had taken her toys away with her.

Chub knew it was okay to cry because Hailey said it was fine to cry if he felt like it but he was too scared right now. He closed his eyes and squeezed himself even smaller and made a mind-picture of Hailey's face and then Prairie and Anna and Kaz. These were his very own mind-pictures, the ones he made himself, not the ones that just opened up bright in his head sometimes.

Chub couldn't help being very scared. But Prairie was somewhere near. He knew that. And Hailey and Kaz were coming because a mind-picture of them popped in between the ones he was making by himself, Hailey and Kaz right here in this room.

There was one other mind-picture he'd seen a few times. But he didn't like this one at all. It was Monster Man.

Monster Man lay in a bed with things stuck in him, white looping lines that went into machines. Monster Man was covered up mostly with white covers and there were lights coming from the machines but they weren't very bright. Where Monster Man's hands should have been were giant white pillows. And his face . . . his face was broken, red and black and pink where there weren't more white bandages. He didn't have any hair, just shiny red skin. His eyes were regular except crazy crazy and there was a bandage where his nose went and a hose thing that went into his mouth hole. But his mouth hole wasn't a mouth. It was red and it was a hole and the hose went in it, and even though the mind-pictures didn't have sounds, he could tell the Monster Man was screaming almost all the time, the mouth hole shaking and the eyes going up inside his head.

Chub wished he didn't have to see that mind-picture.

A long time ago he was a baby and his name was Jacob and he lived in a room with a lady who slept a lot and she was broken and he was always hungry. Then he went to live with Gram and she talked too loud and she was broken too.

But then there was Hailey. Chub wondered how long it would take her to get there. Until she came he would be very small and he would wait.

CHAPTER 13

I WOKE UP WITH THE SUN in my eyes. I blinked and for a moment I couldn't remember where I was, couldn't identify the boxy room with strips of sunlight slanting in on the two beds and the plain brown furniture.

But then I saw Kaz, adjusting the blinds, dressed in the jeans he'd had on yesterday and a worn gray T-shirt that fit him snugly, showing off the muscles in his arms and back.

Then I remembered.

"Good morning," I said, stretching and yawning.

"Hailey." Kaz turned from the window, took a step toward me. Stopped, looking self-conscious, and jammed his hands in his pockets. "Sorry, I didn't mean to wake you up. I brought you some coffee. Bagels."

"What time is it?" I ran my fingers through my hair, hoping that it wasn't doing that sticking-up thing it had been prone to since Prairie had cut and dyed it pale blond.

Remembering that haircut brought all my guilt back. The makeover was only the first of many things Prairie had done to try to protect me.

"Nearly nine. You slept in." Kaz picked up one of the coffee cups sitting on the desk, peeled back the plastic lid and handed it to me. I held it under my chin and let the steam bathe my face.

I was wearing only a thin tank top and my underwear. I pulled the covers up under my arms. I'd have to put my clothes on in the bathroom, maybe wait until Kaz wasn't looking to get out of bed.

I felt my face get warm when I thought of his having spent the night just a few feet away. In a separate bed, but . . . still. We had taken turns in the bathroom, Kaz going first because he was faster, and when I'd come out after washing my face and brushing my teeth and combing my hair, he'd already been asleep, one arm thrown over his head, the other hand clutching the blankets to his chest. I thought it would take me ages to unwind enough to sleep. Prairie and Chub getting kidnapped, running from the scene, kissing Kaz, waiting in the lobby while he checked us in with the debit card—all of it had left me anxious and unsettled. But I didn't remember a thing after getting into bed.

"How long have you been up?" I asked, taking a sip of the hot, bitter brew.

"A while," Kaz said, and hesitated, like he wanted to say something more.

"What?"

"Nothing, nothing. It's okay," he said quickly. "But listen, Hailey, does *Quadrillon* mean anything to you?"

"Quadrillon?" I repeated, confused. "Yeah. It's some sort of high-tech company. They built an office park out east of Gypsum when I was a little kid, back during the whole high-tech boom, because they got the land really cheap plus tax incentives or something. Quadrillon was supposed to move in first. Only that never happened. They went bust right before construction was finished and it's been empty ever since. Sometimes kids go out there, break windows and drink or whatever, and the sheriff comes around. I guess eventually it'll just fall apart and turn into a landfill."

Kaz nodded, as though I'd confirmed a bad suspicion. "That's where they took them. Where they took Chub, anyway. I saw it this morning, right when I woke up. The word *Quadrillon,* with a sort of squared-off four-leaf-clover logo. And then I realized it was a sign on a building. I saw Chub going in the door, over and over. He was with two guys in a car with black windows. Only, the building looks brand-new."

"I don't know how that's possible," I said slowly. "That building was run-down. Unless they could have fixed it up that fast . . ."

"All they would have had to do is lease it under some bogus name and get the power turned on and they could move in, fix up the place. They've had two months. That's plenty of time."

"You're saying they're in *Gypsum*. . . ."

"It makes sense, Hailey. That's where the other Banished are. If they've started up the lab again, they're where they can get all the . . . research subjects they need."

"The Seers," I said slowly. "Rattler would provide the Seers. It might even have been his idea to set up there."

The thought infuriated me: Rattler would be feeding the weaker Banished to the General in exchange for cash, all the while building his own new clan of purebloods.

"Speaking of Rattler . . . ," Kaz said. "What does he look like? Does he have longish brown hair, a scar on his forehead, a little shorter than me?"

"Oh no," I whispered. "You saw him, too?"

Kaz turned away from me, blew out a long breath. "I woke up because I was having a migraine, Hailey. It happens when they come too fast, when the visions . . . take over."

Only now did I notice that his hands shook slightly, that his face was pale and his jaw tight from the pain. "I'm sorry."

"No." Kaz shook his head. "This is good. This can help us. Now we know where to find them."

"What was . . . Rattler doing? Was he at Quadrillon too?"

"I couldn't tell, but he was . . . he looked really angry. He was hitting something with his fist. A wall or—I don't know—a post or something. Over and over."

"Oh." I felt the fear deepen inside me. I'd seen Rattler angry before, but now I wondered who the target was—and given what I had done to him the last time I'd seen him, it could easily be me. As if we didn't already have enough obstacles ahead of us. "You didn't see Prairie? She wasn't with Chub?"

"I don't know. It wasn't, you know, all that definitive. Hey, cheer up, Hailey," Kaz said, forcing a smile. "It's not all bad news. I got us a car."

"What—how?"

"I went to see a friend from school this morning. A guy from the team. I had him come up here; then we drove to my car and switched. He said we can take it for a few days."

"Kaz, you went to your neighborhood?"

"Don't worry, my car was parked on the street. Nobody saw us."

"But—" They could have, I thought. They could so easily have been watching the car. "What if they'd seen you?"

"But they didn't. They *didn't,* Hailey. Look, I know this is hard, and I'm sorry, I'm just so damn sorry to be taking these risks, putting everyone I care about in danger. But I don't know what else to do."

Because it had never occurred to him not to try. I felt my fear retreat a little. Kaz wasn't reckless . . . only determined. And brave. And committed.

I tried to smile at him. "You must have been up for hours. And I didn't even hear you get up."

Kaz looked relieved that I was letting it go. "Nah, you were out. Woke me up with your snoring. I figured I might as well get out for a while."

I felt my mouth drop open, my face flooding with embarrassment. I never snored—at least, Prairie had never said anything, or Chub for that matter.

Then Kaz grinned at me, that big slightly crooked grin, and I knew he'd been kidding.

"So your friend didn't mind?"

"Getting stuck with my clunker?" His grin turned rueful. "He's a good guy, Hailey. You'd like him. And it's not like he traded me a BMW or anything. Don't get too excited, his car isn't a whole lot better than mine."

"I wasn't—I don't care," I protested. And I *didn't* care, not about what kind of car we drove. As nice as it had been to drive with Prairie in the relatively new Camry, it was still a novelty to have a car at all. I had spent most of my first sixteen years riding the bus and walking. "I just, you know, does he know where you're planning on taking it?"

Kaz raised an eyebrow at that and lowered himself to the other bed. He was close enough that I could smell soap on him, and his hair was still a little damp from the shower. So I'd slept through that, too.

"I told him we were going for a drive in the country." He picked up one of the pillows and set it next to him, smacked it a few times. "You know, with cows and all."

I couldn't help smiling. "You say 'cows' like you've never seen one before."

"I've seen plenty. After they've been made into burgers—"

I laughed. "Seriously? How close have you ever been to one?"

Kaz pretended to think. "Football field? A few hundred

yards? They have some in the Lincoln Park Zoo, I think. Why, have you, like, petted them or something?"

"You don't really pet cows," I said, but it wasn't entirely true.

Walking half a mile through the woods in back of Gram's house took you to grazing acreage where Bud Eisle kept half a dozen head of black angus. I'd taken Chub there a few times once he was old enough to make the walk. I picked him up so he could put his hand on top of the cows' velvety noses when they stood at the fence, chewing, showing only the faintest interest. It was before he could talk, but he loved to pet the soft muzzles.

But that wasn't the kind of thing I could explain to Kaz.

"I can't believe I'm going back there," I said. "When I left Gypsum, I thought I'd never go back."

"It won't be forever," Kaz said softly. He reached out for my hand, and I took his—and then suddenly it was the most natural thing in the world for him to tug me gently next to him. He kissed my hair and I let him draw me closer against him, until I could feel his heartbeat through his T-shirt.

This wasn't like yesterday's kiss. This was comfort, and a promise—that he would be there for me, with me. Prairie had made me such a promise. It had taken me a while to believe her—had taken a shared experience of danger, the blood bond of violence—but with Kaz, I simply *knew*.

He wouldn't let me face what waited in Gypsum alone.

Maybe that was why I felt safe enough to say the rest. "You know I was . . . different there."

Kaz murmured, "Yes," tucking my head under his chin

and holding me. I had told him about what it was like to live with Gram—the run-down house, the constant struggle to keep enough food on the table, the stream of drug-buying customers. I'd explained about the Morries—the kids from the Banished families who attended Gypsum High—and the meanness and poverty that defined their life in Trashtown.

What I hadn't explained was where I fit into the high school: how I'd never had a best friend, or any real friends at all; how I'd been mocked and ridiculed for my clothes, my hair, my rusty bike; how the other kids had whispered about Gram, calling her a witch and worse.

I knew Kaz wouldn't judge me for these things. But I was afraid that if I returned, I would lose the confidence that had come at a high price. I was afraid that even though I knew I had changed on the outside—the way I looked and dressed—I would stop believing I had changed on the inside.

"I don't want to go back," I whispered against his soft shirt.

"I know," Kaz said. "But you won't be alone."

Chapter 14

KAZ HAD TOLD THE TRUTH: the car was only a slight improvement over his rusted-out Civic. It was a dented brown Bonneville with a creased bumper. The one splurge his friend had made was to upgrade the sound system with a set of good speakers.

The last time I'd made this drive, traveling in the opposite direction, was the first time I had ever left Missouri. Now the hours passed more swiftly. I was well rested, and music filled the car. We didn't talk much, but occasionally Kaz reached for my hand and gave it a squeeze.

Whenever my thoughts turned to Chub, I forced myself to take deep breaths and remember only good things: the way he laughed with his mouth wide open, showing all his baby teeth; the sound of his voice when he said my name, the one word he sometimes pronounced the way he always had, "Hayee."

I knew that Kaz had to be desperately worried about leaving his mother in Chicago, but he didn't say anything about it. When he caught me looking at him, he smiled as though nothing was wrong. But after we'd been in the car a few hours, his expression changed.

It was a subtle change at first, a tightening of his jaw, a clenching of his hands on the wheel. I watched him carefully and saw that his skin had gone pale and a faint sheen of sweat stood out on his brow.

"What's wrong?"

"Nothing. Much. It's just . . ." He glanced at me, his expression troubled. "I'm getting flashes. Little ones."

"Visions?"

"Not a full vision, not yet. But . . . I probably will. When this happens, it's usually a sign of one coming, a new one. Not the ones I already had, not Quadrillon or Rattler. This one is darker."

He winced, and I could tell it hurt. "What do you see?"

Kaz shook his head. "Nothing specific. It's that damn flicker, the way I get just the pieces. It's water. I think. It's all wavery and shimmering and there's—there's something—someone . . ."

I said nothing. It could be anything. A sink, an ocean, a pan boiling on a stove.

The only thing I felt sure of was that it wouldn't be good.

"Are you okay to drive?" I asked. Prairie had begun teaching me to drive, but so far I'd only got as far as lurching from one end of the apartment-complex parking lot to the other.

"Oh yeah, I'll be fine. Maybe . . . why don't we get some lunch?"

We stopped at a Pizza Hut outside Springfield. I wasn't hungry, but I forced myself to eat; one of the things I'd learned in recent months was that you could never count on your next meal or place to sleep when you were Banished and on the run.

In the car again, Kaz seemed better. The afternoon wore on, clouds lazily drifting in and obscuring the April sun. We drove around Saint Louis, the skyline visible in the distance, the arch beautiful against the darkening sky. I knew that from Saint Louis it was another three and a half or four hours. I passed the time by trying to remember all the good times I'd had with Chub, and then, when that stopped working and my mind pitched and rolled with fears I couldn't contain, I forced myself to think about math, the subject I'd struggled with the most. I imagined the textbook pages, the numbers and equations running into each other, taunting me.

I was so intent on keeping my mind occupied that when Kaz cleared his throat, I was startled see that he was even paler than before, with one hand pressed to his forehead as though he was trying to keep the pain inside.

"Are you okay?" I demanded.

"I think I'd better pull over. Sometimes . . . I think I

might be getting a bigger one. Once or twice I've . . ." He swallowed and blinked hard. "Once I passed out, but don't worry. That won't happen. Yet. I just need to get someplace where I can shut my eyes and rest."

A tall Exxon sign lit up the darkening purple sky at the next exit. A Wendy's and a Long John Silver's shared a parking lot with the gas station, and the lot was nearly full with travelers stopping for dinner.

Kaz bypassed the parking lot, continuing down the road, which narrowed as it wound into the farmland beyond. In the distance the lights of a couple of houses winked on as the last of the sun's glow faded from the horizon. Kaz drove until he found a farm lane with a gated cattle guard, then pulled over and parked in the weeds.

"I'm sorry," he said. "I just need to be away from the lights. Hailey, I'll be okay, really, just give me ten minutes."

I nodded, but already Kaz had reclined his seat and covered his eyes with his hand. I watched him breathe, his chest rising and falling regularly. I wasn't sure, but his color seemed to be a little better already. Maybe if he just let the vision come; maybe he'd been suffering because he'd been resisting it. I knew the feeling. When I had first felt the urge to heal—when a girl had got hurt in gym class—it had been nearly impossible to resist. As I waited to put my hands on the girl's broken skull, to say the ancient words, an urgency that was almost . . . painful overtook me. But was it pain? No, it was just a *wrongness,* a deep and unmet need that grew sharper and more demanding until I gave in to it.

Maybe Kaz's visions were the same way.

I sat as still as I could and watched him. Five minutes turned into ten, the time passing achingly slowly. I wondered if he had fallen asleep, and decided that might be for the best. It grew harder to see him in the dark, but I knew he was there next to me and that was good enough.

Down the road, the cars came and went from the parking lot: hungry travelers, weary families, people trying to get to their next destination. Nothing sinister, nothing out of the ordinary.

There was really no reason for the anxiety that had been gnawing away at me ever since we'd left Chicago, a raw and seething layer underneath all my other fears.

Kaz rested. I waited.

CHAPTER 15

RATTLER SHIFTED ALMOST IMPERCEPTIBLY on the wood shelf that served as a seat. Next to him, Derek startled, caught napping. Derek was no good at waiting. He had no patience. Rattler bit down hard on his disgust: the Banished blood was weak indeed in Derek, but he was all Rattler had for now.

But the future—ten years from now, there'd be new blood all around town. Young, strong boys and girls with at least one full-blood parent—and a few with two. When Rattler grew old, his many children would make him proud, and there would be grandchildren and great-grandchildren, all Banished, all strong and determined, and they would live well here. They would take their rightful place as the leaders of Gypsum; they would drive fancy cars and live in big-ass houses, and the biggest one of all would be the one he would build for him and Prairie.

He and his Prairie, they would grow old together; they would look out their front door and see what was theirs . . . *their* land, *their* town, just like the village of their ancestors. If something displeased Prairie, Rattler would blast it sky-high; if someone made her unhappy, he would remind them by force who was the leader of the Banished, who had returned them to their rightful glory. No one would make Prairie unhappy twice. If they did, Rattler would make them taste their own blood as they died.

They would see. They would all see. So far, they hadn't understood, and maybe, just maybe, some of that was his fault. He had failed with Prairie once, but she had been under the influence of that other one, of Mr. Chicago, with his slick ways—he saw that now. He hadn't seen that then, when Mr. Chicago had offered Rattler money to turn Prairie and Hailey over. But that was then and this was now.

Rattler worked up a gobbet of spit and let fly, narrowly missing Derek's boot. Derek was wise enough not to say anything; he just moved his foot out of the way.

The memory disgusted Rattler: Mr. Chicago with his stack of hundreds, peeling, peeling, peeling, waiting for Rattler to signal when it was enough. Well, he'd taken the man's money—why shouldn't he?—but it was never enough. It would never be enough! And see what had happened to Mr. Chicago, who had thought he could buy Rattler? Charred and dead, burnt up in his own squalor, a fitting end.

Not that there was anything wrong with making a little

money from the gifts. No, nothing wrong at all. He needed cash. He needed capital. Others had stepped up to take Mr. Chicago's place, and Rattler had showed them, hadn't he? He had taught them a blood lesson they would not forget. Now they would respect him. He would set a high price for their services . . . his and Hailey's and Prairie's. And he would bring the others, the Trashtown riffraff who possessed only a shadow of the gifts, let them experiment on his lesser brethren, let them play their games with the piss-weak stock, even as Rattler was beginning to rebuild the clan.

He would be like a broker; he would be the businessman he'd always known he could be. His sons would take up the yoke someday. He would teach them, train them. And in his home, Prairie would raise the girls, and they would be strong and beautiful, like her. It would be as it should be.

Next to him, Derek cleared his throat. "We been out here—"

"Shut up," Rattler said automatically. "Drink."

Rattler knew that Derek had a flask in his pocket; there was rarely a time when Derek *didn't* have a flask in his pocket, topped off with cheap whiskey. That was okay, though; what he needed Derek for didn't require quick reflexes. Rattler just needed an extra hand in case the boy gave him any trouble. The boy was expendable; Rattler had armed himself with the Ruger just in case, but he hoped not to use it. Just put the boy on the road and send him back, that was all that was called for.

But he needed the girl. Because the girl was the next step to Prairie. And she was his firstborn, a Healer like her mother, so she was rightfully his as well.

She had to know it too. Otherwise why was she coming back here? Had to be scared, seeing what she'd seen. He understood that. A sheltered girl like her, all she knew was the home her granny had made for her, that retard boy they'd taken in, the mongrel that ran in the yard. Her granny didn't let her talk to the Morries, and that was good and right. The few times Rattler had seen one of the Morrie boys talk to her, he'd made sure it was the last time. He might not have been the most involved father, but a girl didn't need that, anyway. She needed a dad who looked out for her, who knew what was right and what was wrong. Rattler did the right thing when it was important. He kept the boys away. He would make sure that when the time came, it was a pure-blood boy who came to call, and no other.

She must have known that. Because where, after everything that had happened to her, was she coming to find safety? Back here to Gypsum. Oh, Rattler didn't have any illusions that she was coming to *him*. She had in mind to come see a girlfriend maybe, a favorite teacher. Who knew with girls? They were delicate things, emotional things. Hell, he thought ruefully, rubbing the socket around his scarred eye, they could be quick and unpredictable, and a man had to be on his toes around them.

But now she was on her way back. Rattler had seen it with his blind and spinning eye that morning as he'd lain in bed: he'd seen the car, the girl, the boy, the Exxon sign lit up in the sky above them.

Derek took a dispirited swig from his tarnished flask and returned it to his pocket. He didn't bother offering it to Rattler. Everyone knew Rattler didn't drink. He never had, even when they were kids, Rattler and Derek and Armand and the rest of them skipping class to smoke behind the Elks lodge. Even then Rattler knew drink was poison; it was what had led so many of their fathers away from the Banished. Drink made them lazy, distracted them, and then they married outside; they sired their bastard broods and drank and did drugs and pissed away their pride and their birthright.

No more.

"If they was comin', they'd be here by now," Derek said, a little more loudly, disgust in his phlegmy voice. The liquor gave him courage, a cheap and deceptive kind of courage, but one that had to be dealt with all the same. True, the man had let Rattler take over the old house on his dead pappy's land, and Rattler owed him for that, maybe, though a man who'd live in his mother's trailer instead of cleaning up the mess his own father had left behind wasn't much of a man in Rattler's book. But Rattler had taken something from Derek, and he would remember that when it came time for splitting up the spoils. Derek would be taken care of.

That was the future. Now was now.

Rattler moved fast. His hand shot out and seized Derek's ear and twisted it, and as Derek squirmed and mewled like a puppy, Rattler twisted harder and forced Derek's head around so he would have to look across the field to where night was etching a layer of purple-black on the fading glow where earth met sky.

"Guess you don't know nothing," Rattler said softly as an old brown sedan pulled slowly off the road and came to rest a few feet shy of the cattle guard.

CHAPTER 16

How could we have slept?

I woke with my head resting against the cold glass of the passenger window, the night thick and black on the ground, only Kaz's outline visible as he slept next to me. I had been dreaming something awful, something disturbing enough to wake me: I'd been back in the locked room in the lab, fire raging behind me, the zombies rising from their chairs, staring at me with their unblinking eyes, their rotting, impassive faces and coming at me. Their feet on the floor clacked and slapped, a rhythmic sound as they came closer and closer and—

But the sound, the clacking, did not stop, even though I was awake. It was in my ear, on the glass, and I jerked away from it, too late seeing that there was something, some*one*, out there, silhouetted against the star-dotted sky. I grabbed

Kaz's arm and yanked it hard, trying to force his name from my lips. But fear had stolen my voice.

"What is it?" Kaz woke instantly. "Hailey? What's going on?"

"Outside," I managed to croak, and then I gasped, because there was another figure on *his* side of the car, this one thin and stooping. Then a brilliant beam of light shone in our faces, blinding me.

"Open up." It was a rasping gravel voice thick with the drawl of Trashtown. My father's voice.

"Rattler," I whispered, clutching Kaz's arm harder. As if to confirm the thought, the tapping resumed, gently now, but the light shone pointedly on the barrel of a gun, the thing Rattler had been using to tap the glass. And it was pointed at me.

"Come on now, Hailey-girl," Rattler crooned, almost a singsong. "Come on outta there. We're goin' for a drive."

"He won't shoot me," I said. But he would shoot Kaz without a second thought.

Kaz knew it too, because I could see him hesitating, reaching for the keys dangling in the ignition, trying to figure out whether he could get the car in motion before Rattler took a shot.

The grinning figure on the other side, leering through the window, seemed to make up Kaz's mind. Slowly, he took his hand off the keys.

Rattler had known we were coming.

He and Kaz, both Seers, were plagued with visions of the

things that stirred them most, the things that they held dearest or that threatened the greatest harm. That was how it always worked. Kaz had seen the Quadrillon sign because Chub was there. Rattler, though, cared most about Prairie. I lowered the window a crack. "She's not with us, you know."

Rattler's expression didn't so much change as drive over a speed bump. For a flash of a second, it was shot through with anguish and even worry, something I'd never seen on his face before. "I know it," he muttered. "Now get out."

Kaz reached for my hand and gave it a squeeze, and then we both got out. My mind raced, looking for ways to fight back, to escape, but Rattler seized my arm roughly and guided me toward Kaz and the other man. Rattler was much stronger than me, and the other man held a gun loosely at the small of Kaz's back as they headed for the road. A car drove past in a blur of headlights and spun gravel; the people inside probably didn't even see us walking along the ditch beside the road, and even if someone stopped and inquired whether everything was all right, I was sure Rattler had a reply at the ready. Help wouldn't come in that form.

We walked toward the lights of the gas station and fast-food restaurants ahead, not even a quarter of a mile away. I shook my head in disgust as we came within fifty yards of the giant Exxon sign: choosing to stop here in the shadow of this sign was like sending Rattler a postcard inviting him to come find us.

I'd made another rookie mistake. I kept pretending that I

could stay a step ahead of all the dangers that surrounded us, and I kept failing. First I'd led the General's men straight to us. And now Rattler. I couldn't keep letting things like this happen. I had to be sharper, think faster.

At the edge of the Long John Silver's parking lot was a big old sedan sagging on its wheels, and Rattler and the other man led us to it. In the parking lot's bright lights, I got a better look at the man and realized I knew him; he had been one of Gram's regulars. Derek Pollitt. He'd been one of the quieter ones, never putting a hand on me or even joking with me, and for that I was grateful. He opened the passenger door for Kaz and then got in the driver's seat.

Rattler opened my door, but before he released my arm, he stood looking into my face. It was the first good look I'd had of the eye I'd stabbed, and it was a transfixing sight. The skin below the eye was rimmed with a red ragged scar. The eyeball was milky and pale, and it seemed to spin as Rattler stared at me, but surely that was an illusion.

I looked away first, and Rattler laughed, a harsh, bone-chilling sound. "Aw, don't be that way with your daddy," he said. "You and me, we got off on the wrong foot, after all this time. We both got a little makin' up to do, I'd say. Now, I'm not going to hold this against you."

He pointed at his wrecked eye. It was true—Rattler didn't look angry, only slightly amused and . . . somehow very much alive, sparking with the manic energy I'd always associated with him.

"You and me, we got the same goal here," he added as he

pushed me gently into the car. "We're gonna get your auntie back. And then we're gonna set out to restore the good family name."

I slammed the car door, trying to shut out the sound of his laughter.

CHAPTER 17

I KNEW WHERE WE WERE GOING after just a few miles, when Derek took a right at the fork in the road past Sugar Creek. We were headed for his daddy's land, mostly poor clay soil that had yielded stingy crops of alfalfa and soybeans until Mr. Pollitt died eight or nine years back. Everyone thought Derek, the Pollitts' only son, would take over, but instead he leased off what he could and let the rest go fallow and moved in with his mama at the far edge of Trashtown. Derek's mama hailed from the Banished; his daddy did not. Mrs. Pollitt was long divorced from her husband and was at first more than happy to house and feed her only child and wash his clothes. I guessed it had gotten old fast, as Derek never seemed to be able to hold on to a job more than a few weeks at a time.

Next to me, Kaz gave me a reassuring smile and took my

hand in his. Derek, who was leaning over the seat, keeping an eye on us, guffawed. "Aw, check it out, young love."

"Leave 'em alone," Rattler snapped. "'At boy's got pure blood in his veins, which is a damn sight more'n you can say."

I saw a look of hurt pass across Derek's dull face, but he shut up.

I hadn't realized that Rattler knew Kaz was Banished, but it made sense. I was still getting used to the ability to sense other Banished, the curious magnetism that was like a stirring of the cells when they were near. Prairie had explained that it would become second nature before long; Kaz had said that for him it was like yet another layer of vision, on top of the reality that everyone else saw and the pictures that occasionally flashed through his mind.

I closed my eyes and willed myself to be open to it, and sure enough I got a faint sense from Derek, but the connection with Rattler was almost overwhelming, like an invisible thread binding our destinies. It combined fear and familiarity with something else, something inevitable and dark but also part of me.

For my first sixteen years, I had believed that my father was dead, as Gram had wanted me to believe. How many times had I wished for a father to rescue me from Gram's run-down house, to protect me, to cherish me?

And now, bizarrely, I had what I had wished for. "He won't hurt us," I whispered to Kaz.

We turned onto a weed-choked gravel drive leading into

a hollow, where the old Pollitt farmhouse was tucked behind a stand of poplar trees.

"Home, sweet home," Rattler announced, but I was certain I saw Derek flinch as he looked at the old board-framed house, the sagging porch with its toppled flowerpots spilling dirt.

The padlock on the front door was brand-new, gleaming in the beam of Rattler's flashlight as Derek fumbled in his pocket for the key. Inside, there was a smell of decay overlaid with bleach. Rattler snapped on the lights and I saw that we were standing in a plain square parlor that contained only a couple of straight-backed chairs, a threadbare sofa and a dusty braided rug. Near the door were half a dozen trash bags overflowing with junk. Someone had been cleaning, preparing for our arrival, no doubt.

This was meant to be our new home.

"After you," Rattler said grandly, but Kaz didn't budge.

"Come on, now, boy, don't be like that. You'n me, we're practically kin, you bein' full-blood and all."

Kaz and I followed Derek through the parlor and up the stairs. He turned on the lights as he went. None of the bulbs were very bright, and the dim light added to the gloom of the place, illuminating torn wallpaper, worn carpets, stained and cracked ceilings.

Upstairs was a narrow hallway with a bathroom and three closed doors. Two of them bore shiny padlocks just like the one on the front door.

Rattler stepped in front of us and opened the first one.

"This was supposed to be your auntie's room," he said. "But you can use it till she gets here."

When he turned on the light, I stopped short, at a loss for words.

Rattler had fixed the place up with care, a prison for his beloved that he'd filled with the things he thought she would like. The bed was neatly made up with a faded quilt, but there were extra pillows and lace-edged sheets. An embroidered runner had been draped on the little table next to the bed, and a jar of flowers stood by a dish filled with small polished pebbles. I had once had a collection like that in my own room, stones that had been tumbled smooth from a thousand years in the bottom of Sugar Creek.

Clothes were folded over an armchair pulled up to a wooden desk. They were brightly colored, things I knew Prairie would never wear. She favored dark, plain shirts and pants, gray and black and navy blue; in the stack I saw fuchsia and pink and red and orange, the colors of a summer flower bed.

A sadness stole through my heart, surprising me. Had there been a day, when Rattler and Prairie were children, when these had been my aunt's favorite colors? As a little girl, playing with the other Banished kids, had Prairie ever been carefree? Had she and my mother picked flowers and chased dragonflies and splashed in the creek before things went bad, before they started school and learned how much the townspeople hated Trashtown, before the other children refused to play with them? Had Prairie once owned a pink dress? Had she worn it for the high school boyfriend who she'd long ago lost?

I looked around the rest of the room. The old furniture had been polished, the floors scrubbed. A stack of shiny new magazines lay on the little desk next to a photo in a silver frame.

I stepped closer. In the frame was a photo of two kids, around eleven or twelve years old. A girl with dark hair almost down to her waist balanced on a rock in the middle of a creek, a look of intense concentration on her face, the bottom of her jeans wet. A tall wiry boy leaned toward her from the edge of the photo, almost out of the frame, grinning and reaching for her, all summer-tanned skin and white teeth and too-long hair, pants too short and sleeves barely reaching his wrists, a boy who was growing toward manhood as fast as he could, who even then wanted nothing more in the world than he wanted that girl.

I swallowed hard and glanced at Rattler, and for the first time ever, he refused to meet my eyes. "Don't you wear her things, now, Hailey-girl," he muttered. "Derek, go on in that other room and get what-all I bought the girl."

Derek was back in moments with a stack of jeans and T-shirts, new and shiny with the price tags still attached, which he laid on the bed without a word.

"Had to guess at your sizes," Rattler said. "And I ain't got anything for you, son, but we can get that took care of. I didn't guess I'd be hostin' you here or I would have been prepared. Now come on, we got a phone call to make."

CHAPTER 18

I SHOULDN'T HAVE BEEN SURPRISED to see the setup on the kitchen table—Rattler's cell phone was attached to a sleek compact speaker—except the technology was so incongruous with the worn, sparse old furnishings.

"Y'all'll be able to hear 'im just fine," Rattler promised. "And more important, he'll be able to hear you, too."

"I need a li'l somethin' before we start," Derek said, and I noticed that his hands shook as he opened an old metal cabinet and took out a bottle. He splashed liquor into a brown coffee mug and took a greedy drink.

"Hell, you don't even need t'be here, you don't want," Rattler said impatiently.

"It's my house," Derek protested, half angry, half forlorn.

Rattler nodded and his lips curved in a slight smile.

"That it is, buddy," he said softly while he waited for Derek to cap the bottle and put it back.

When we were all sitting down, Rattler picked up the phone and thumbed a few keys. Instantly we heard the ringing as though it was right in the room; almost immediately the call was picked up, but after the click of the connection being made, there was silence.

"It's me," Rattler said, not bothering to mask his drawl. "Your good friend Rattler Sikes. And this had better be the man in charge, or I'm hangin' up. I don't mean to speak to nobody else."

"Don't hang up," a deep, clipped voice said. "This is Alistair Prentiss speaking. I am the man in charge, as you say. Thank you for calling, Mr. Sikes."

"Well now, it just seemed like the right thing to do, after y'all sent them folks to pay me a visit th'other day."

Prentiss coughed slightly, and Rattler caught my gaze and winked.

I felt a shiver of nerves run through my body. I'd expected Rattler to be furious, given the way I had injured him, the damage I'd done to his eye. At best I'd expected him to trade me to Prentiss, to sell me for whatever he could get them to pay. But he'd treated me well enough since finding us pulled off the road.

I didn't trust him, of course. I figured he'd go after Kaz first, maybe see what he could get for him, a Seer with a great deal of power, before starting to negotiate for me.

"About that . . . ," Prentiss said. "You do understand, Mr. Sikes, that was only business."

Rattler laughed, a hearty, rich laugh from deep in his chest. "You sent a couple guys to drag me out of my own home, threatened to put me in the ground if I didn't go with 'em. That all in a day's work for you?"

"Yes, Mr. Sikes, in your case. But it seems I underestimated you."

Rattler had been sitting tipped back on an old kitchen chair, but at Prentiss's words he slammed the chair down on the floor and laid his forearms flat on the table, glaring at the speaker as though it had offended him. "Hell yeah, you did. And your hired men paid the price. That don't speak to a whole lot a balls, you ask me."

"Indeed. I won't make that mistake again."

Rattler let the moment lie, his thick black brows knit in fury. Slowly, he relaxed, getting control over his emotions. Across the table, Derek looked from Rattler to the speaker and back, mouth slightly open as he tried to keep up with the conversation.

"So, Prentiss, I got somethin' I believe you want. Got the Healer y'all were trying so hard to get your hooks into, little gal called Hailey. Say hello, Hailey."

I pressed my lips together. I didn't want to speak.

"Aw, come on, now, sweetheart. Just say hello to the man, nothin' more. He don't need to know any of your . . . private stuff. This is just business, like he says."

Rattler's expression stayed neutral as he spoke, but he was staring at me intently, and I knew exactly what he meant by "private stuff"—like the fact that I was his daughter. No one knew that besides Prairie and Anna and Kaz.

"It's true," I muttered. "My name is Hailey Tarbell."

There was no response from Prentiss, and I imagined him assimilating this new information. In my mind's eye he was a large man, only slightly diminished by age, broad shouldered and muscular, wearing an immaculate uniform with medals on his chest.

"Ms. Tarbell," he said after a long pause. "It is an honor to make your acquaintance."

Acquaintance—I bristled at the word. He made it sound as though we had met at a party in a fancy restaurant, as though we were shaking hands, when he had been behind a plan to imprison me, to force me to create zombies. I remembered how Prairie's eyes used to waver with fear whenever she mentioned the General; she was even more terrified of him than she was of Bryce.

"Now, Prentiss, I've got one other person here might be of interest to you," Rattler continued. "Young man's a full-blood."

"Well, that *is* good news," Prentiss said smoothly. "I am assuming you refer to Kazimierz Sawicki. I have already had the pleasure of making Mr. Sawicki's acquaintance, though only over the phone. I do look forward to meeting him in person."

If Rattler was surprised, he covered it well. "You'll meet him if'n when *I* say so."

"As you and I have discussed in the past, I am sure we can

work out a mutually beneficial arrangement wherein you provide . . . subcontractors, for a generous finder's fee."

"Yeah, for your *research studies*," Rattler said sarcastically. "Aw, now, don't go gittin' ahead of yourself. Boy's doin' just fine here, for now. I'm sure you realize that my terms are up for a major renegotiation. My people are worth a hell of a lot more to you than the few thousand bucks you threw my way last time. I mean to make sure you appreciate that fact before we do business again."

"Mmm," Prentiss said. "I do agree that these are precious resources, of course, Mr. Sikes, and we do intend to compensate them—and you—appropriately."

"Now hang on a minute," Rattler said, his voice going deadly. The manic fury that always swirled underneath the surface threatened to emerge; he sat up straight and gripped the edge of the table in one strong hand. "I don't think you're in a position to be callin' the shots here."

"Oh, did I forget to mention—I'm sorry, Mr. Sikes, there's one additional piece of information that may make you a bit more amenable to my proposal." His voice was cold, almost bored. "You see, a little earlier today, several of my . . . associates stumbled onto an unexpected opportunity to bring a person of interest into our little family. And we're delighted to have her, of course."

"What are you saying?" Rattler demanded, the color draining from his face.

He knew, even before Prentiss answered.

"We've got Prairie Tarbell."

CHAPTER 19

THE NIGHTSHIRT RATTLER HAD BOUGHT ME was too big, and it flapped around my knees while I got ready for bed. Rattler had at least let me use the bathroom by myself, waiting outside in the hall with his chin ducked down, almost like he was embarrassed to be there. I took my time brushing my teeth. I needed to think, and I wasn't looking forward to being locked into "my" room for the night.

"Come on now, Hailey-girl," Rattler's rough voice growled through the door. "Don't be takin' all night. Big doings tomorrow."

I knew he hadn't thought of anything else since Prentiss had told him they had Prairie. Neither had I. Hearing Prentiss's cold, arrogant voice on the phone only deepened my horror that I had led him to her and Chub.

Still, I hoped Rattler's obsessing might make him careless.

I wasn't about to tell him anything about her capture. I guessed he was waiting for a vision to give him direction, and I didn't plan on helping.

I splashed water on my face and blotted it dry with the thick, soft towel Rattler had given me, then opened the door. Rattler grunted and led me back to the room he'd prepared for Prairie. He pointed to the bed. "See you don't muss it up, now. It ain't meant for you."

After he locked me in, I slid under the blankets. The floral sheets were clearly expensive, soft and silky. The pillowcase was embroidered and edged with lace. Everything was too frilly for me—flowers and lace and pastels—but I could imagine Rattler choosing the finest things he could find, storing them up for the day he brought Prairie home.

I lay in the bed, unable to sleep. Thoughts of Chub and Prairie and Anna circled through my mind, my fears alternating with schemes and plans I abandoned one after another. Finally I got out of bed and snapped on the delicate lamp that sat on the bedside table. I went to the wall that joined my room with Kaz's, and tapped gently, putting my mouth close to the plaster.

"Kaz," I said in a low voice. "Can you hear me?"

In a few moments there was an answering knock, and then the murmur of his voice—too low for me to make out his words. I didn't dare speak any more loudly. Rattler and Derek were downstairs, and while I guessed that Derek might keep drinking until he passed out, I knew Rattler never drank.

I looked around the room, wondering if there was anything I could use to cut into the wall, maybe make a small hole behind a picture or under a flap of wallpaper, but there was nothing.

Still, I felt better knowing that Kaz was close by. I got the pillow and comforter from the bed, lay down on the floor next to the wall and knocked one more time to let him know I was near. After that, I was asleep in moments.

Rattler's voice woke me. "What the hell are you doing down there?"

I sat up slowly, rubbing sleep from my eyes. It took me a moment to remember what I was doing on the floor as I stared at a pair of well-used black work boots.

I scrambled to my feet, drawing the comforter around me like a robe. Rattler beckoned impatiently. "Come on down here. I got something to tell you."

I had to beg him for a few minutes in the bathroom, and I could hear him tapping his foot on the floor the entire time. If I'd had any illusions that his attitude toward me was softening, they were laid to rest when he made a point of showing me the handle of his gun above his belt. "Git on, now."

Kaz sat at the table with Derek, eating a bowl of cereal with a banana sliced on top. A tall glass of orange juice and a cup of coffee sat next to his bowl. In front of Derek were a bottle of aspirin and a glass of water, though he sat up a little straighter when we came into the room.

"Hailey," Kaz said, and pushed back his chair.

I wished I could touch him, hug him, but Rattler got there first and shoved Kaz back into the chair as though he was a child rather than a two-hundred-pound man. Kaz was strong, but Rattler was too.

"Sit back down, boy," he growled.

"Are you all right?" Kaz asked, never taking his eyes off me. I nodded, and Kaz slowly pulled his chair back up to the table.

"Derek. Git 'er something to eat."

"Tell her to git it herself, I ain't—"

"Get up, Pollitt," Rattler ordered as he took a seat and motioned to me to do the same. "Get off your lazy ass and earn your keep."

Derek reluctantly got up, clutching his temple and shaking his head. "I don't see why she cain't, why they both cain't fix their own breakfast, they're both—"

"You leave the thinking to me," Rattler said, cutting him off. "Don't tax yourself, seein' as you probably kilt a few thousand more brain cells last night."

Derek refused to look at Rattler while he got up and stumbled to the counter, where he got another bowl and poured cereal and milk into it, muttering to himself.

Rattler waited until the bowl was set down in front of me, then rested his elbows on the table and looked from me to Kaz and back, narrowing his eyes shrewdly.

"You seen anything new, boy?" he asked. I'd been wondering the same thing, but I prayed Kaz would keep it to himself if he had.

But Rattler didn't wait for an answer. "'Cause I just had me a nice little view of Hailey's aunt. Also a couple a guys gonna wish they'd never laid a finger on her, time we're through."

My heart skipped. "Did they hurt her?"

Rattler's expression tightened with fury, his black eyebrows knitting together, his lip curling and his jaw going tight. "No. Not yet. And they ain't gonna get the chance."

"Did you see where she was?" Kaz asked.

"Hotel room," Rattler said. "Chicago. I could see the skyscrapers out of the window. Up on a high floor, got her locked up like a damn bird in a cage."

His fury was even stronger than before. I thought I knew why: a hotel room with a view like that would be expensive—far more luxurious than anything he could provide for her.

The irony—that he wanted to imprison her just as Prentiss's men had, that only the location was different—seemed to escape him.

"Do you know which hotel?" I asked.

"Not yet," he muttered. "But I will."

"What are you going to do if you find her?" Kaz demanded.

"Not *if*, boy—*when*," Rattler snapped. "I'm gonna bring her here, where she's meant to be. We're going to be a family. Me, her . . . my daughter."

He hooked a thumb at me, his words giving me a chill.

"Aw, don't look at me that way, girl," he added, noting

my reaction. "Gonna have sisters before long. You're gonna help raise 'em up, a whole mess a Healers. I'm gonna make things right around here, put things back the way they're supposed to be. No more giving away our destiny, our bloodline."

"How are you going to do that?" Kaz demanded. "Round up Banished women and lock them up here? You're gonna run out of room pretty quick."

The blow that sent Kaz crashing onto the floor came so fast that I didn't even see it, but suddenly Rattler was standing over Kaz with a boot on his chest. "Don't you sass me again, boy," he spit, and I realized that even without the gun he held in his hand, he was more than a match for Kaz. There was something almost inhuman about his coiled energy, his sheer power. Kaz was strong, his body tuned and hardened by lacrosse, but he was not a fighter, and in a match with Rattler, he would lose.

"It ain't your place to question me, boy," Rattler continued in a voice that was eerily soft. "I run this house. I will lead the Banished. I know where the blood runs strongest, and I—"

"What about me?" Derek demanded in a whining voice. His skin was pale and clammy and there were purple bags under his eyes. "You promised me a woman, you promised—"

"Yeah, right," Rattler said smoothly, his expression flattening out as he turned to Derek. I realized that Derek had to be really stupid not to know he was being lied to. To me, it was obvious . . . but then again, I was the man's daughter. There was more to the blood than I wanted to acknowledge. Rattler would never be my dad, but in fathering me he had passed on more than pure Banished blood: I was able to read him, sense his moods. "You'll have your pick, Derek. Any woman you want."

"I better," Derek mumbled, taking a drink of his water, some of it dribbling down his chin. "I just better."

Rattler took his boot off Kaz and offered him a hand, which Kaz refused. As Kaz got to his feet, Rattler shrugged. "There may be a place for you, son, once you realize I'm your best shot here. Hailey stays with me. You work with me, maybe you can stay too."

He turned away, so he didn't see the look Kaz gave him. But I did, and Kaz's silent fury mirrored my own feelings.

Rattler was strong, and he was smart. But we would find a way to be stronger and smarter.

CHAPTER 20

AFTER RATTLER LEFT, his old truck spinning gravel as he peeled out onto the road, Derek got more and more agitated. I suspected that it was because he wasn't drinking. As much as I knew he wanted to, he was too afraid of Rattler, who had made him promise to watch us around the clock and keep us out of trouble.

"Ought to just lock y'all up in them rooms upstairs," Derek muttered several times.

The minutes ticked by. I had found a stack of old *Time* magazines in a drawer, and Kaz and I tried to read them while Derek played with the change from his pockets, pushing the coins into patterns on the table. I thought I'd go crazy from boredom, but I didn't want to provoke Derek into following through with his threat. At least I had Kaz for company as long as he let us remain downstairs.

A little before noon, there was a knock at the front door.

"What was that?" Derek said, his hands shaking with nervous energy as he set his coffee cup down harder than necessary, bitter brew sloshing onto the table.

I could see the front door of the run-down house from the kitchen. Staring through the gloomy, dusty sitting room, I thought I could see it tremble on its hinges as the sound came again: a methodical, rhythmic pounding.

"We don't got to answer that," Derek said. He swallowed hard, pushing his chair back from the table and brushing at his lap. "We wait a bit, why, they'll leave like as not, whoever that is."

"Mr. Pollitt," I said in a low voice, "if someone's come all the way out here, odds are they aren't going to give up just because we don't answer the door. This house . . . your family's home . . . it's been, uh, empty for a while now and I'm guessing everyone knows it. Let's say they saw us drive in, maybe they're worried about a break-in or something, being a good neighbor and checking it out. If you don't talk to them, they're going to make some calls. Trust me on this, they're not going to let it lie."

No matter who was there—a neighbor, a traveling salesman, someone from the phone company—there was a chance it could turn into an opportunity for escape, as long as Derek didn't panic and do something crazy. The farm road was thinly populated, and even a little extra traffic—Rattler's and Derek's driving back and forth to town as they stocked and outfitted the house—might easily have been noticed. I wondered how Rattler could have expected any different—

people in Gypsum knew everything about each other—but then I realized that he just didn't care. He meant to keep me and Prairie here under lock and key as long as necessary, but he was banking on it not taking all that long, on our staying willingly soon enough.

Despite everything—despite Prairie rejecting Rattler over and over when they were children, despite her leaving town with no intention of ever returning, despite his having brutalized her sister and fathered me, even despite my having tried to kill him—he had faith in his vision of us as a family. A family that would swell with more children and grow to include any Banished he deemed worthy—those whose blood was pure. The rest would be relegated to the grunt work, like Derek.

Rattler's belief in his vision gave him power, and his power terrified me. We would need every advantage we could find to fight him.

"Hailey's right," Kaz told Derek. "Do you want me to get the door?"

"Stay there, boy," he ordered Kaz. "I guess this is still my damn house, I'll answer my own goddamn door." With his hand on the knob, he turned and glared at us. "Y'all keep quiet. And ease on back where they cain't see you."

We complied, flattening ourselves against the kitchen wall, out of sight of the front door. Kaz stood close behind me, his warm breath on my neck. As soon as Derek turned his back, I peeked around the corner. I wondered if I should scream when Derek opened the door, yell that we were being held hostage, but Derek had his gun in his hand, and I didn't doubt he'd use it—on the visitor, if not on us.

He opened the door and I could see a tall figure standing in the bright morning sun, but I couldn't make out his features in the blinding light.

"Yeah?" Derek said. "I help you with somethin'?"

So it wasn't someone he knew, a neighbor or someone from town. My dread grew as I wondered if Prentiss could have found us already, if even now a team was circling the house, covering all the escape routes.

But the visitor said nothing. He didn't appear to have a weapon; his hands hung loose at his sides. After a moment he took a step, crossing the threshold and stopping inches from Derek.

"Hey, what the . . . Holy shit," Derek yelped, and suddenly he stumbled backward, scrabbling to aim his gun at the intruder. "Don't you come any closer!"

But the man took another step, out of the pool of sunlight and into the cool dimness of the house, and as my eyes adjusted, I saw that something was terribly wrong.

"I'll shoot, I'll shoot you!" Derek said, but his hand was shaking badly and he was practically tripping over himself trying to get away from the man.

That was when the smell reached us. It was the sickly-sweet smell of dying flesh, of infection-racked tissue losing its battle with rot and gangrene. Bile rose in my throat and I thought for a moment that I would throw up on the kitchen floor, but Kaz tightened his hand around my arm.

"Is that—" he said, but then a shot rang out and Derek staggered backward and the man stopped coming and wobbled on his feet, a new hole in his soiled white button-down shirt.

Derek had shot the . . . thing, the thing that Prentiss had sent here, the thing that had once been a man but was now just a body. And not a fresh body, by the looks of it.

Once before, I had seen the undead close-up, when I had accidentally stumbled into their storage room next to the lab. The fire was raging by then, burning down the entire building, but the zombies sat motionless in their chairs until they saw me, and then they stood up and came for me. They cared about nothing else; they had been told to kill, and that was all they meant to do. I fought them with everything I had, but it was a losing battle until Kaz found me and threw himself into the struggle, and together we pushed and shoved and kicked and bit—oh God, yes, I even sank my teeth into their dead cold flesh—and we managed to lock them in there finally to die completely, to burn and burn until only piles of bones remained.

As I stood frozen, staring in shock, I realized something that had escaped me in the lab: I would never be able to look at one of these creatures and forget what they had once been. This one had been a man, a young man, with a full head of longish hair that was bleached at the tips; his hair still looked normal, like it might have once been something he was proud of. But the rest of him was ruined. When the dying are healed, they do not live forever in the undead state: what remains rots and disintegrates, though more slowly than ordinary dead flesh. This man had been not-dead for a while, long enough that his skin had started to crack and peel in some places; in others it was swollen and black and oozing, literally rotting away. His eye sockets sagged, his unseeing eyeballs a sickly yellow, and his mouth hung open, his lips shrunk back against his gray teeth so it looked as though he was leering at me.

Except he—*it*—didn't look at me at all. Once it regained its balance, it took another clumsy step forward, toward the center of the house, ignoring Derek, who was trying to aim again, gibbering with fear.

"Don't you even— I shot you, damn it—stop right there—"

He still hadn't figured it out. He managed to steady his aim and shot the intruder again, hitting it this time in the gut, blowing a hole that left the fabric of its shirt ragged and flapping, but this time it barely bothered to register the blow, instead swiveling and heading toward Derek.

I tried to scream, but somehow the sound got stuck in my throat. I had to warn Derek, tell him he was no match for the killing machine that had been cobbled together from the ruins of a human, but as I struggled to form the word *no,* Kaz dragged me backward, his powerful arms circling me from behind, my feet sliding across the old scarred wood floors. He was saying something, yelling into my ear, but I couldn't make it out over Derek's screams as the thing wrapped its blistered, peeling hands around his neck and started to squeeze.

Derek fought hard for a man who'd already given so much of his life over to alcohol and despair. I watched him struggle, flailing at the thing's hands, trying in vain to kick at its legs. Right until the end, Derek gave his all, but finally he sagged backward, his head lolling to the side, and the thing let him drop to the floor, the formless bag of bones that had been Derek coming to rest in an awkward pose next to a spindly side table.

A scream filled the air, and when the thing took two more steps into the foyer, I realized that the sound was coming from me, but I couldn't stop. As the zombie shuffled toward the center of the house, I saw what was strapped around its waist, half a dozen cylinders taped in place, a cord leading to one of its hands.

Bombs.

And then I understood.

Prentiss had somehow found this place—this humble house in which Rattler planned to begin building his empire—and he meant to burn it to the ground. It made a crazy kind of sense: Prentiss couldn't compete with Rattler's powers, his visions, his ability to summon and manipulate the Banished. He couldn't force Rattler to work for him or to provide fodder for his experiments; he'd already tried to recruit him, offered Rattler money to bring the Banished to him.

When that hadn't worked, he'd sent a team to capture Rattler at his house. Only Rattler had a vision that they were coming. He lay in wait, sly and strong and quick-witted, for Prentiss's men—and then he killed them all.

So Prentiss had switched tactics. Somehow he knew that

Rattler was hiding out in Derek's father's house, so he sent in one of his zombies to blow it up. He expected Rattler to see it coming, but he knew that Rattler couldn't stay on the run forever. He expected Rattler to slip up eventually, and when that day came, Prentiss would be there to capture him and force him to do his work.

But Prentiss didn't know everything about the visions. They couldn't be predicted or controlled. They showed danger and destruction and pain and loss before it happened, but Rattler didn't care about the shack and he didn't care about Derek, not really. And more important, his mind, his entire *being*, was focused on Prairie right now.

Any visions Rattler had would be of her.

Kaz was trying to drag me toward the back door, my feet slipping along the splintered wood, but when I understood what was going to happen next, I grabbed his hand and ran. I glanced back once to see the thing that had been a boy with surfer hair stop and hold the cord up in front of him, his eyes unfocused and uncaring, his grotesque face indifferent, and then Kaz threw open the screen door and pushed me out into the bright morning and I stumbled on the leaning steps and Kaz was dragging me across a weedy yard with a clothesline strung between a tree and a shed that was missing a door and the last thing I noticed as he threw me to the ground next to the shed was the sweet smell of soil and mold and a pile of flowerpots mounded in the shade.

And then the world exploded.

CHAPTER 21

THE FLASH CAME FIRST, a white-yellow blink, followed a second later by a boom that shook the earth and blasted through my skull. I felt Kaz frantically trying to cover me with his body but I pushed him off, twisting to see the little house burst, shingles flying and foundations splintering, a cloud of yellow flame blooming from within. A piece of window sash sailed into the yard and crashed inches from where we lay, its jagged edge impaling a fat hosta plant. Glass splintered from the window and rained down along with charred and smoking debris. My head echoed with the force of the blast, and though I could see Kaz's lips moving as he screamed at me, all I could hear was a dull roar.

I let him pull me to my feet and only when I stood did I notice that he was bleeding. Bright, pulsing blood was literally pouring from his forehead and he stumbled, never letting go of my hand, and touched his skull, his fingers coming away glistening red. He swayed and I tried to catch him in my arms, but he staggered backward and we both fell into the shadow of the shed, coming down hard on the packed dirt, his wounded head bouncing on the grass.

"Kaz!" I screamed as his eyes fluttered and rolled up in their sockets. I could hear my own voice but it was as though it was coming from a distance, as though someone else was screaming as I ran my fingers lightly along the jagged tear in Kaz's skull and felt broken shards of bone.

No. No. This couldn't be happening, not to Kaz. My knee pressed into something sharp and I realized that debris thrown from the explosion had hit the garden pots and cracked them into dozens of sharp-edged pieces. Whether it was a piece of pot or something from the house that had struck Kaz didn't matter now. I felt my heart seize with fear and shock but I forced myself to brush Kaz's hair out of the way and gently check his wound.

The urge to heal grew within me, a longing so powerful it was as if my body itself transformed from flesh into pure need. The words filled my brain, an ageless whispering chant, and they were on my lips and I had to clamp my mouth shut, biting my tongue, to stop myself from saying them. My fingers thrummed with the electric desire to touch Kaz as a Healer, to knit together his broken skull, his torn flesh, to still the blood flow and repair the tissues.

But I couldn't let myself. Not yet.

Not until I knew if Kaz was too far gone.

Because if I healed him after the life left his body, he would not come back as the boy I loved. He would become just like the thing in the house, the thing that had come on an errand of destruction and now was torn to bits by the blast, shreds of bone and skin whose soul had long since left. If Kaz passed on before I tried to heal him, I would create a zombie.

"Kaz, Kaz," I screamed. "Can you hear me?"

For long seconds, he lay motionless, his eyes unseeing. My soul shattered with grief at the thought of losing him, of losing the one person besides Prairie who really saw me when he looked at me, who understood who I was and loved me anyway. I felt my eyes fill with tears, hot and stinging, and as I blinked, one fell on his forehead and trailed into his blood and mixed with it. Where it had fallen, the ragged torn skin blurred and skimmed over.

Even my tears were a Healer's.

I seized Kaz's hands and squeezed them. "You have to show me now," I said, choking back my sobs. "If you're alive, you have to show me, I can't, I can't . . ."

But he said nothing at all, and I couldn't feel his pulse, couldn't find the thread of his life, and the unfairness of it nearly cleaved me in two.

I'd come so far only to lose everything. Chub had been stolen from the streets where we'd finally thought he was safe. Prairie had been taken too. And now Kaz lay broken on the hard-packed earth of the miserable town I'd fought so hard to leave.

I couldn't escape them all on my own, Rattler and Prentiss and his men. I needed Kaz. Together we were more than a couple of scared kids; together our history and our gifts made us strong. I lowered my face to Kaz's and kissed his bloodied forehead, his parted lips.

And he stirred. Just a little, a tremor, a twitch—but I knew. He was still there.

"Hailey," he breathed, licking his cracked lips. His eyes flickered and the life came back to them and he sought me with his gaze. I felt him squeeze my hands in return. "Is there . . . anyone . . ."

"It's just me and you, Kaz," I said. I didn't want to upset him further, but I knew he needed the truth. "Derek couldn't have survived that."

He shook his head with effort. "No . . . I mean . . . anyone out front . . ."

But I had seen enough; now that I knew that Kaz still lived, I gave myself over to the powerful pull of my gift. I let my eyes drift shut and touched my fingertips very gently to the edges of Kaz's wound, feeling him wince in pain. The voices in my head swelled and rushed through in a current of near-melodic phrases and I spoke the words, murmuring softly while the gift gathered strength and my hands moved of their own volition.

Under my fingertips I felt the flesh knitting, the shattered skull fragments melding together. Heat and energy and power were all focused into the touch. As I chanted the ancient words, the energy flowed from within me to him. *Take what you need of me,* I willed the forces at work on his wounds. *Use me, use me up.*

I had healed Kaz once before, when fire and bullets had threatened to take him from me. Then my gift was new, and I was unsure and afraid. But each time I healed, my touch grew more assured, and the words came more easily to my lips. When the last broken bits of his skull had smoothed back together, when I felt only his sweet, regular breath against my wrists, I laid my head on his chest and rested, feeling the reassuring rise and fall, and slowly my other senses returned.

First I noticed the smell: a horrible combination of char and chemicals and smoke. I blinked several times, my vision momentarily blurry, as it always was after a healing, but as it cleared, I made out the house behind the wall of flame and smoke pouring from its center. The trees that lined the drive were unharmed, their branches waving in the billowing smoke. On the ground a few feet away lay a shred of flowered fabric that I recognized as part of the curtains that had hung in the kitchen. Farther away were broken dishes, the face of a clock, half a splintered chair, all spread out as though a giant had sprinkled the ruins of the house from his hand.

My hearing was returning quickly. Healers were stronger than other people; we never got sick, and though we couldn't heal each other, wounds that would kill ordinary people were nothing to us. I was grateful for my strength and resilience now; though I had healed Kaz, I knew we would both need our strength for what lay ahead. We needed to get away from here, before Prentiss sent someone to make sure his zombie had carried out its task. We'd been dealt an incredible stroke of luck in that no one had seen Rattler bring us here last evening; darkness had surely helped. But we couldn't count on that luck lasting.

I felt Kaz tense up, his muscles going rigid. My heartbeat quickened with fear. "What is it? Are you all right?" But before he could speak, something pressed into the small of my back.

"Stand up slowly, hands where I can see them," a hard, clipped voice said. "You first, Hailey."

I didn't know the voice. But I knew that we were in big trouble.

CHAPTER 22

CHUB PUT DOWN HIS BOOK. The glasses lady was talking to the lunch man. The lunch was on the plate with the green cover, just like before. Chub didn't know what it was even though the glasses lady asked him could he guess. He said macaroni, but it smelled like chicken dinosaurs. Hailey made him chicken dinosaurs sometimes and he liked them and he didn't like anything here. He didn't like it here and he was scared a lot and he didn't like to go to the bathroom in this bathroom. He didn't like it here but now he had a mind-picture and he put down his book.

If the glasses lady knew, she would make him say but Chub didn't want to say. It was the Monster Man and they were making the Monster Man play the bad games too. Not the same games because there was no hiding thing and the glasses lady wasn't there. Chub couldn't see who was there but someone was making the Monster Man play a game.

With numbers. There were numbers. Chub couldn't see the numbers but he knew there were numbers. At school Miss Kathy said to count and Chub could count a lot. One two three four five six and more and more numbers. Sometimes you could put the numbers on the magnet board and sometimes you wrote the numbers on a pad. And the Monster Man had numbers too and he was hiding them inside his head.

Chub knew about that. Sometimes he hid things in his head. For a long time he hid his words there and nobody knew. They weren't a secret, they just didn't come out. Then Hailey helped him let the words out of his head and that was good but sometimes he still liked to hide things there. Sometimes it was for fun and sometimes he just didn't want to tell.

The Monster Man didn't want to tell before, but now he wanted to tell the numbers. The mind-picture went wavy and then it was gone and then it was back and Chub went by the bookshelf so the glasses lady didn't see him watching the picture. They were doing something with the lunch. He put his book on the shelf and took another book down and put it on the floor. The Monster Man kept the numbers in his head but now he was telling the numbers. It wasn't a game. No, not a game. He wanted to tell the numbers because it could help someone.

The Monster Man was a helper. He was so scary before

but now Chub saw he wasn't as scary. His face wasn't a monster face now. Someone had fixed his face. He didn't hurt as bad. He wanted to be a helper.

Helping was good. But Chub wasn't going to tell the glasses lady. Helping was good, but she didn't know that.

CHAPTER 23

THEY COVERED OUR FACES with loose black fabric hoods, but that didn't matter. I knew exactly where we were going. Gypsum wasn't that large, not even when you included all the farms that circled the edges of town, the fields full of early-season soybeans and alfalfa and corn, the grazing acreage and the rich land along the creek. Growing up here for sixteen years, with no friends and no brothers or sisters, no mother or father to entertain me, I had explored every inch of town on foot and occasionally on a broken-down bike I'd found abandoned at the dump.

All my exploring had been cut short when Chub had arrived. Then I'd begun living for him, and our exploring was limited to the fields and forest around our house, paths and secret hideouts known only to me, places where a little boy could walk and play.

But I still carried the map of Gypsum in my mind, and as the car navigated the gravel drive and then the pavement of the roads, leaving the smoking ruin of the house and Derek's body for the fire team whose sirens we heard in the background, I knew exactly where we were.

They were smart, our captors—a pair of men so like the ones who'd first come after me and Prairie a few months earlier that it was almost funny. Rent-a-Thug, I thought; but who knew how many more of these guys Prentiss had on standby? If anything, this team was even better trained than the first one; maybe Prentiss had stepped up his demands after the first team was killed in Gram's home when they tried to kidnap us.

Mustache, as I'd nicknamed the one who'd pressed his boot into my back, was tall and dark-skinned and seemed to be in charge. He gave us short, clipped orders as his partner, who had a shaved head, a freckled red face and a tattoo around his arm, cuffed our hands behind us and forced us into the back of the car.

As we rode, I leaned against Kaz, his chin resting on the top of my head, and traced our path in my mind. They took the first turn on a dirt road that looped around the back of a drainage pond and crossed a brackish swale before heading through a mile or so of new-planted fields and coming out on State Road 9. By then I could hear sirens in the distance; the smoke cloud above the Pollitt land could probably be seen all over Gypsum. Soon neighbors would head over to see what had happened. It was more excitement than Gypsum usually saw in a month, and half the town was likely to show up, along with the entire sheriff's department and the fire crew from Casey. Meanwhile the sedan turned down hidden drives and doubled back and looped, and only by concentrating hard did I follow its path—even though I'd known from the start that it would eventually make its way to the abandoned business park.

By the time it hit the last stretch, I could no longer hear the sirens. We parked, and when my door was opened, all I heard was the buzzing of a few crickets. We were led up a walk, and I stumbled once or twice, not being able to see the ground in front of me. A whoosh of an electric door opening was followed by a blast of cool air.

We took a walk down a long hallway, and then we were guided through one last door and our hoods were taken off. We were in a conference room, its long narrow table and the dozen chairs around it looking brand-new, the whiteboard pristine, the projection system humming softly above us. At the head of the table was a tall, broad-shouldered man in his sixties. He had a neatly trimmed beard and a buzz cut, and he gave us a tight smile.

"Welcome." Prentiss—the man whose voice we'd heard on the phone.

"Where's Chub?" I demanded.

He held up a hand and chuckled. "Slow down, young lady. You've barely arrived; why don't you get comfortable? I'll have some sodas brought in. Surely you would like to refresh yourselves after your . . . unfortunate adventure."

150

He gestured at my scratched arms and filthy, ruined shirt, at Kaz's disheveled hair and the faded bruises and cuts that remained after the healing.

"I know exactly where we are, you know," I said furiously. "You could have had those guys drive me around for hours and I'd still know we were in the business park. I mean, it's not like there's anywhere else in town that's got this kind of money poured into it."

"Ah, that," Prentiss said, inclining his head in a parody of an apology. "Procedure, I am afraid. You'll learn, Hailey and Kaz, my young friends, that discipline is at the heart of every successful venture. Procedure. Chain of command."

"What branch of the services did you come from?" Kaz demanded. "Was it even ours?"

Prentiss scrutinized Kaz, one eyebrow raised. "You're questioning my patriotism, young man?" he said softly.

Kaz glared silently, and Prentiss made a show of pretending to remember something, snapping his fingers in the air.

"Oh dear, I forgot—you lost your father in the Gulf War. A brave man, Tanek Sawicki. He was proud of his citizenship, Kaz, was he not? Proud of fighting in the army of his adopted nation?"

Kaz said nothing but I could sense his fury escalating. I reached for his hand and held it tightly until I felt him respond, his grip relaxing slightly. I needed him to be focused, to remember why we were here—not to avenge his father's death, but to rescue his mother and Chub.

"Only . . ." A look of fake sorrow passed over Prentiss's

features. "There is more to the story, I am afraid. Details of his last engagement that were classified. Have you wondered what really happened that day, Kaz?"

Kaz did not speak; he just held my hand more tightly.

"As I thought. Kaz . . . I was, during that chapter of our nation's history, close to, shall we say, the heart of the intelligence community. I had access to information that was never made public. I could—"

"Tell me, you bastard," Kaz hissed. "If you know anything about my father, tell me."

"No," I whispered. I knew what Prentiss was doing—trying to draw Kaz's focus away, to break him down, to weaken our bond, to turn him against the government so that he would agree to participate in the research. A Seer like Kaz—he would be of great value to them.

Wait a minute. A Seer like Kaz . . .

Prentiss had been there, with access to classified information about the troops stationed in Iraq. . . .

"You knew," I said accusingly. "You knew his father was a Seer."

"Ah, Hailey, you impress me again," Prentiss said, clapping his hands in delight. "There was an experimental psychic viewing program that was begun back in 1988, when we first found evidence of psychic prodigies among the new recruits. Kaz, your father was far more gifted than any subject before or since. When word of his abilities reached me, I immediately called for his transfer to a more stable location, where he could enter our program safely. But . . ." He waved his hands impatiently. "Paperwork. Red tape. Bureaucracy. In the end, I was not able to transfer him soon enough. Not before that terrible day in Al Busayyah. Your father did not have to die there, in the dirt. It was, if you care to know, the last straw in my frustration with working from within. The reason I decided to go . . . independent, you might say."

I glanced at Kaz. His features were frozen in hatred. Grief would come later, I suspected, when he was alone.

If Prentiss thought he could sway Kaz with this story, he was mistaken. Prentiss might have tried to save his father, as he claimed, but it was only so Prentiss could use him. And we both knew it.

"Now we have an opportunity to work together, Kaz." Prentiss pressed on. "You can save the lives of American soldiers like your father. We'll begin with a few simple tests. Get to know one another, so to speak, before we begin exploring your marvelous gift. And then I'll share what I know. As two colleagues might. Because that is what I want you to see me as, Kaz. Your colleague, your comrade, with a shared goal. Not to mention the promise of handsome rewards."

"So now you're bribing him?" I demanded, enraged. "Are you insane? Why would he ever agree to help you?"

Prentiss frowned at me, eyes narrowed. The good humor disappeared from his expression. "You would do well to remember that we also have Jacob. Oh, excuse me . . . Chub, as you know him."

His words chilled me. "What do you mean . . ."

"Jacob Alan Turlock. Born at home, rushed to Casey

General Hospital to deal with complications at birth. Fetal alcohol syndrome and . . . but you don't want to hear the whole list now, do you, Hailey?"

They knew everything. They knew where Chub had come from. They knew things about him that I had never known, and I realized that it wasn't only Kaz who was under their thumb.

Prentiss had me.

"As I thought," he said softly. He signaled to the men who'd brought us here. "We have so much to talk about. Why don't you two freshen up, change into clean clothes, have something to eat? And then we will talk again."

"I have nothing to say to you," Kaz said. He shook off the guard's hand as he stood.

"Oh, I very much doubt that," Prentiss said mildly. "I foresee many interesting conversations ahead for the three of us."

"I have nothing to say to you either," I said.

"Is that so?" Prentiss gave me his full attention, drilling me with his cold stare. His eyes were slightly bulging and watery. "There are carrots and sticks, my young friends. I am a civilized man, a peaceful man, at heart. A merchant. I would far prefer to employ carrots. Rewards. We can do smart business together and you will be handsomely compensated. You can have a rich and rewarding future with us. Or . . . you can fight me. But then I will use a stick. And trust me on this: those who have felt the force of my stick wish they had never challenged me."

CHAPTER 24

PRENTISS WAS PREPARED to be more than generous with the carrots, if the accommodations he provided for me were any indication. The room I was led to had a broad window overlooking the fields rolling away to the east. Far in the distance I could see a stand of black willows lining the bend in Sugar Creek. A mile or so after that, the creek took a turn to the south and joined up with Beaver Creek and eventually flowed into the Lake of the Ozarks.

I had never been to the Lake of the Ozarks. Kids at school were always talking about family trips to the campsites and motels that lined the hundreds of miles of shoreline. They talked about days spent lying on the beaches, with their trucked-in sand and weedy bottoms, paddling canoes and going to waterslides and eating barbecue. There were waterskiing and wakeboarding, sunburns and mosquitoes and car stereos playing loud.

And I had never experienced any of it.

I took a hot shower and dried off with a fluffy towel, then dressed in the clothes that had been left for me. They were plain—black pants and a black silky T-shirt—but the quality was very fine, and the fit was almost perfect. I dried my hair and treated my cuts with antibiotic ointment I found in the medicine cabinet. I looked through the cosmetics that stocked the shelves, wondering who had chosen them— probably some junior member of Prentiss's staff, a woman selected because she was young herself or because she had a daughter my age. For a moment I felt myself softening and then I realized I had to steel myself against everyone here. I couldn't afford to forget for a minute that they had kidnapped Prairie and Chub, that they meant to put us to work making zombies.

I slammed the medicine cabinet, leaving the cosmetics untouched.

Then there was nothing to do but wait. The sun was high in the sky, a weak sun filtered by filmy clouds that signaled rain later in the day. Far off in a field of corn I saw someone making his way down the rows with a ground sprayer, but he was too far away for me to see his features.

By now, the local farmers must have noticed the activity at the office park. No matter how careful Prentiss was, he couldn't hide the deliveries of all the equipment and supplies. Or the staff arriving from around the country, possibly even around the world, the best in their fields, the ones who could be swayed by salaries far above what they could earn in the public sector or—for those who valued their work above money—who would do anything for a chance to work on the cutting edge.

But how hard would it be to convince the people of Gypsum that the activity at the park was innocent? No one would scrutinize the details too closely if money was coming into the community. If Prentiss was smart, he'd seed the town with payouts for everyone. Sign up for food delivery from the local distributors. Hire landscapers, laundry service, waste service—all the while posing as some company that manufactured computer components or medical supplies. He could pay off a few inspectors so they wouldn't look too closely at the research labs and paint a few trucks with fake logos, and as long as the money kept flowing, no one would ask questions.

Sometime down the line, people would start to wonder why there were no jobs for locals, why no one ever saw the inner workings of the facility—but Prentiss was probably betting that by then he would have everything he needed, and he could exit the town as stealthily as he had arrived. His reason for locating here was to be close to the Seer population, but maybe he thought he could win them over with his endless cash resources. And he was probably right. Once the Banished men got used to a steady paycheck, they would probably be just as willing to relocate for Prentiss as the rest of his staff was.

There was a knock at the door, and after a moment's hesitation, I opened it. Standing in the doorway was a woman I hadn't seen before. She was around forty, thin, with brown hair pulled back in a severe ponytail. She wore a pressed white lab coat, glasses, a slash of red lipstick and a smile that looked like she had to work at it. "I'm Dr. Grace. It's nice to meet you, Hailey."

I ignored the hand she held out for me to shake. "Where's Chub? Where are you keeping him?"

Her smile faltered and she withdrew her hand. "I should tell you that there are security cameras throughout the building. We are being observed, and if you do anything to threaten my safety, armed personnel will be here in a matter of seconds."

"Good to know," I said sarcastically. "I guess I won't use my Vulcan death grip on you, then."

She didn't speak as she led me down the hall. I looked at every door we passed, hoping to catch a glimpse of Chub, but they were all closed. It smelled like new construction and fresh paint, and I guessed this wing had been turned into a residence for the staff.

Including the reluctant ones, like me and Kaz—the ones who had to be locked in.

We descended a set of stairs below ground level to a cafeteria. The smell of cooking made my stomach growl, and I realized I hadn't eaten since breakfast. A dozen people lined up with trays, and others sat at tables in pairs and small groups, eating and talking. I couldn't help being impressed that they'd gotten all this up and running so quickly, an entire self-sustained community within the office park. There was no reason for any of the staff to venture outside the buildings. Trucking in the food and supplies had to cost a fortune, but money didn't appear to be a concern to Prentiss.

"We'll be in the private dining room," Dr. Grace said, and pushed open a glass door to a bright and sunny room. The long table in the center was laid with white linens, fresh flowers and china. Prentiss and Kaz were already seated at one end, along with a man dressed like Dr. Grace.

Prentiss stood when we entered, followed quickly by the other man. Reluctantly, Kaz stood too; I could tell he was battling between good manners and not wanting to give Prentiss the satisfaction of complying with him.

Once we were inside, I saw that there was one more person in the room: the guard from earlier, the tall one with the mustache, stood by the door, his expression impassive.

"Lunch will be brought in shortly," Prentiss said as Dr. Grace and I took our seats. "I hear there's fresh catfish today. They do it very well here, with a light breading and a lemon sauce. I'm sure you'll love it. And if you don't, they are happy to accommodate special requests."

"Cut to the chase," Kaz said. "You said you'd tell me when Hailey got here. What do we have to do to see Chub?"

Prentiss's expression turned thoughtful. "I'm afraid he is on a . . . slightly different meal schedule, at the moment. Dr. Grace feels that Jacob—uh, Chub—will benefit from a program of limited contact with others as—"

"He's probably terrified," I interrupted, realizing as soon as the words were out of my mouth that that was exactly what the General intended. He was isolating Chub to force him to cooperate with the testing in exchange for the simplest of comforts—a lap to sit in, a story to be read to him. Or a chance to see me, now that I was here.

"I won't eat until you let me see him," Kaz said, folding his arms across his chest. "You'll have to knock me out and put a tube in me."

"Oh dear, there's no need for all this drama." Prentiss sighed as a young woman wheeled a cart into the room. "Have a nice lunch, dear boy. If you're worried about being poisoned, you can take your pick of any of the dishes. Thank you, Mavis," he added as the server began setting salads at each place. "If you'll just—"

A muted chirping caused him to frown. He pulled out a sleek phone and spoke quietly. "Yes? . . . You're sure? Where? . . . How did he . . . Cutler *and* Greybull, you're positive?"

I could make out the frantic tone of the voice on the other end, but not the words.

I knew it had to be about Prairie. She was the only loose end still out there; the rest of us had all been brought here. How long had it been since Rattler set out for Chicago? Nine hours? Ten? Just about long enough to reach Chicago if he'd driven fast. Just as Rattler had known where to intercept me and Kaz, he could have known where her captors were going to stop for gas or lunch.

I glanced at Kaz, who was watching me with his eyes

narrowed. His expression told me he was thinking the same thing I was.

"Dead?" Prentiss's face, which was already tight with anger, twisted into a mask of consuming rage. "How the *hell* did you let that happen?"

My pulse spiked with fear. Had Prairie been killed in a fight with Prentiss's men? Or Rattler? Or had she somehow managed to fight back—and win?

"How fast can you get there?" I heard fury building in Prentiss's tightly controlled voice. "You've got half that. Secure the bodies. Call Gurz; he'll assist with the troopers and police. I'm on my way; I'll be right behind you."

He hung up without further comment. Mustache lowered his hand from his ear and I realized he'd been listening in, patched into the call. Already he was dialing another number. "Code black," he muttered.

Prentiss took a deep breath and shut his eyes for a moment; when he opened them, his placid expression was nearly restored, and he managed a brief smile.

"I'm terribly sorry, but I have been called away on an urgent matter. Hailey, Kaz, I leave you in Dr. Grace's capable hands, and we'll speak again tomorrow."

"Is she all right?" I demanded. "Prairie, is she all right?"

The General didn't answer.

CHAPTER 25

JASMINE, RATTLER THOUGHT. She smelled like jasmine, the first white blooms of spring on the shrubs that still grew along the edges of Trashtown, long after the person who'd planted them had died and been forgotten.

He closed his eyes and let himself remember: a long-ago July morning, before the sun scorched the sky, chasing Prairie into the hedge. He just wanted her to stop screaming, so he hooked a foot around her leg and sent her facedown in the dirt under the jasmine hedge. He slid down next to her, rolled her over, saw the scratches on her tearstained cheeks, held her wrists so she couldn't lash out at him. He wanted to make the tears go away, wanted her to stop screaming so he could just tell her what was inside him, the way she made him feel, but he didn't know the words.

So he'd ground her hands into the dirt and made her cry harder, all the while breathing in that spring-bright smell of jasmine.

But they weren't kids anymore. They were grown, and Rattler was a man, and she was his woman and she *would* mind him. His hands were in her hair and he seized a handful and yanked hard enough to jerk her head back.

"Hush your mouth," he growled, but she hadn't said anything. She just stared at him, her green eyes throwing sparks, her lip curled in a sneer that let him know she wasn't half broke yet.

For a minute he felt rage rise in him and he wanted to break her, devil be damned, right here in a dried-up wash somewhere in central Illinois. He didn't know this land, didn't know who owned the tidy white barn a quarter mile away, the row of black walnut trees, the hound baying at the end of its chain.

What he did know: the blood on their clothes had been spilled by his own hand. And he'd spill more if more bloodshed was what it took. He'd do anything for Prairie and for the life they were meant to lead.

It had been almost too easy to take out the ones who'd had her locked up. His spinning eye showed him the way, told him what to do. He shot the first man right through the door. The other didn't have time to get out of the chair. But Rattler didn't notice the beat-up mess of a woman in the corner until she came at him like she was hungry for the bullet, dragging her chained-up chair behind her. Rattler didn't want to shoot a Banished, but she wouldn't stop and she wouldn't stop, no matter he told her to stay back.

That messed him up. He hadn't wanted to shoot her, and as she gurgled her last breath, Rattler felt his rage at Prentiss growing stronger. The man kept taking what was his, and Rattler's wrath was a living thing now, a hungry beast that would tear his enemies limb from limb, that would roar so loud that everyone in Gypsum would hear. The ground would disappear in a lake of blood before he let Prentiss win.

He raged and he beat his fist on the wall in that fancy hallway, and that was how the last one got away, a fast-moving thing with long curly hair. She darted out the door and down the hall and disappeared into the stairwell, and Rattler could catch her easy, but then he saw Prairie through that door the curly-hair one left open. Prairie with her pretty mouth open a little like she was saying his name, Prairie with her fancy shoes and her fancy hair he wanted to mess up with his hands, Prairie who knew him like no other. He let the curly-hair one go. He took Prairie because Prairie was his, and they rode the elevator together, and when it stopped on the other floors, Rattler stared down every man or woman who wanted to get in the little box with them. The box was not big enough to hold him and his feelings. The world was not big enough to hold him and Prairie and his feelings.

But first things first, which was why he'd pulled off the road for a little talk once they'd got good and far out of the city and night had come down to hide them. A talk and then a night's rest, that was what they needed.

"Now, before I give you this, girl," he said to Prairie, "you git to thinking on what you're gonna do. 'Cause seems you and me got the same goal here, least in the short term. We're going after Hailey and the rest. We work together, we might just save that little bastard child and them Polacks. You shoot me down, they don't stand a chance."

Prairie still said nothing, but she gave him the tiniest of nods. Slowly, reluctantly, Rattler eased off her, slid his hands from her hair, leaned back in the driver's seat.

Then he handed her his favorite gun.

He watched her settle it into her hands. It looked good on her, warm steel shimmering silver. When she lifted it and pointed it at him, he allowed himself a smile. She was brave, a natural hunter. The blood ran as thick in her veins as it did in his.

"Now listen well," he said as she raised the gun until it was inches from his crazy spinning eye and sighted down the barrel. "I seen water. I seen more dead before tomorrow's done, and I seen you by my side. Mind me well, girl, and do as I say."

He turned away from her then and eased his seat back, fixing to get his sleep. "And put that thing down. You know you ain't gonna shoot me—not tonight, anyway."

CHAPTER 26

PRENTISS AND MUSTACHE HURRIED OUT of the cafeteria as alarms sounded elsewhere in the building. Several other staffers abandoned their lunch and followed, barking orders into cell phones.

Dr. Grace stared at us nervously. She and Kaz and I were alone in the dining room now. "Everything is fine," she said uncertainly. "I'm sure they will be back soon. Meanwhile, why don't we, um, take a tour? I can show you the recreation facilities. We have a gym, sauna, a volleyball—"

"I don't care about any of that. I just want to see Chub," I interrupted.

Kaz caught my eye. He shook his head subtly and I followed his gaze to the ceiling above the door. Mounted in the corner was a tiny security camera. I glanced around the rest of the room but didn't see any others.

Dr. Grace was shaking her head. "You know that is not possible, not without Prentiss on-site. But I'm sure he'll be back by tomorrow, and once things are back to normal, I can suggest a visit. Perhaps you can observe me working with him."

Kaz mouthed something, but I couldn't make out the words.

"Um . . . ," I said. Dr. Grace looked at me suspiciously. "Have you been spending much time with Chub?"

"I am his principal contact, yes," Dr. Grace said. "I am in charge of his testing, as well as his daily regimen."

"When you say testing . . . ," I said, trying to keep her talking. Kaz had a plan, and I needed to keep Dr. Grace from noticing. I forced myself to look curious. "What exactly are you looking for?"

"Well, as you undoubtedly already know, Chub is a high psychic with a strong tendency toward precognition," she said, her features relaxing as she warmed up to her subject.

Kaz raised his glass to his lips and drank the rest of his tea. As Dr. Grace talked about Chub's abilities, he slammed the glass down on the edge of the table, smashing it into several pieces. He catapulted from his chair, picking up the largest shard and pressing it against Dr. Grace's throat, wrapping an arm around her neck so she couldn't move. He gripped the glass so tightly that it cut into his own flesh, and blood ran down his arm in glistening red rivulets. It was just like what had happened with Jess, and I froze at the memory.

"Lock the door, Hailey!" he said, and I snapped out of it, forcing myself to move. I threw myself at the heavy glass door, pushing it shut. There was a loud click as it latched into place. Through the door I saw the cafeteria erupt in commotion as staff raced toward us, weapons drawn.

"Here's what's going to happen now," Kaz said, talking fast. "I'm guessing that door is reinforced and it'll take a few minutes for anyone with the right code to get down here."

"But, Kaz, we can't—" I stopped myself before I said it: *Can't leave here, not without Chub.*

Kaz stared deep into my eyes and said, "Trust me, Hailey."

Only once before had anyone said those words to me. It was the night Gram was shot. Prairie and I were careering across a moonlit field in her old Volvo, pursued by Gram's killers in a much faster car. Until that moment, I'd never believed I could trust another human being, but I closed my eyes and did my best. And we survived.

Now, for the second time ever, I put my life in someone else's hands.

"Open this door!" one of the men yelled. His voice was only slightly muffled by the glass.

"I'll kill Dr. Grace!" Kaz shouted.

I knew that it was a bluff, that Kaz wouldn't take a life unless he was defending himself or someone he loved. But he looked convincing. The sharp piece of glass had grazed the tender skin of Dr. Grace's neck, and her blood trickled down and mixed with Kaz's, dripping to the floor as he held her immobile.

The men outside conferred in whispers.

"Empty the cafeteria," Kaz ordered.

The guards hesitated; then one barked a command and the remaining diners filed out, followed by the kitchen staff.

"Now set your weapons against the wall and lie on the floor," Kaz yelled. "When we come out, we will take your guns. You will not get up. You will remain where you are and order the hallways to be cleared. We will take one of you with us, and if we see anyone as we exit the building, we will kill both you and Dr. Grace. Do you understand?"

The shorter guard, who seemed to be in charge, shook his head. "No way."

"I said I'd kill her," Kaz roared, jerking Dr. Grace around so that the guards could see her terrified face.

"Then do it," the guard said. "The outcome is the same either way. You're screwed."

Of course.

Dr. Grace's life was not a big enough bargaining chip. They would rather let her die than risk losing the two of us, a Seer and a Healer. After all, we were the keys to all the work they were doing here. No matter how brilliant Dr. Grace was, they could always find another scientist.

They couldn't find more Healers or pureblood Seers, and they knew it. More important, Prentiss knew it, and I had no doubt he had communicated his priorities very clearly. Life here was not sacred.

Kaz's gaze met mine and I knew he had reached the same conclusion.

"If you're going to do it," Dr. Grace said, her voice shaking, her eyes squeezed shut in fear, "please make sure you kill me clean. If you don't . . ."

It was a moment before she managed to complete her sentence. "If you don't finish me, they'll turn me into one of them."

I knew it was true. They wouldn't waste a dying woman. They would force me or Prairie to turn Dr. Grace into a zombie.

That was it, the end of hope. As Kaz looked at me with terrible regret, the shard of glass clattered to the floor.

He didn't need to tell me that he wouldn't—couldn't—kill Dr. Grace. But the way she sagged against the wall with relief made it clear that she hadn't been sure.

Outside, the two guards smirked. We had played our last card. Now they knew our limits, and we were no longer a threat to them.

I thought of Rattler, so far the only one of us Banished to stand up to Prentiss and win.

I wondered who was the greater evil: Prentiss, who thought nothing of creating and selling human killing machines, or Rattler—my father—who wanted to turn us all into a twisted kind of family in which love was laced with fear and tainted with spilled blood, whose destiny came from a cursed patch of earth in Ireland.

Rattler was a killer. But his life and his history were bound forever with mine. In that moment I couldn't help being glad he had seized Prairie from Prentiss. At least now she had a chance.

Dr. Grace crossed her arms tightly over her chest and

pressed herself into the wall as though she wanted to disappear. The taller man, who had a thick drawl and a Texas Longhorn tattoo on his forearm, tapped his gun against the glass. "Open this door."

The shorter guard, who was wearing a tight-fitting shirt that showed his powerful arms, shook his head. "We need to just leave them in there until Prentiss gets back."

"With her? Are you crazy?" Texas said. "There's no telling what they'll do."

"You saw that—they didn't kill her when they had the chance."

Texas snorted. "Yeah. But there's no telling how they'll feel in an hour, you keep them locked up. I'm bringing 'em out."

"No." Biceps stepped between Texas and the door. "With Prentiss and Barbieri and the others gone, I'm next in command."

Texas looked surprised, then pissed off. "Really? What are you, Employee Number Thirty or something? Bryce brought me in on the ground floor. Anyone's going to take care of business until they get back, it's me."

"In case you haven't noticed, Bryce is a crispy critter," Biceps shot back. "No one gives a shit what he thinks."

Texas pushed Biceps out of the way and started to open the door, but I was focused on what he'd just said: *Bryce is a crispy* . . .

Is. Not *was.*

Not dead. Alive.

CHAPTER 27

I LOOKED AT KAZ and saw that he had heard it too, his eyes wide with surprise.

We had seen Bryce taken from the building, seen the burnt flesh, the missing shoe, the sheet covering his body—but what if he had somehow lived? What if someone had covered him to disguise his still being alive? Prentiss, with all his connections, might have gotten to him first. Prentiss had access to the best technology available: could it have been enough to save Bryce?

But there was no time to think about it now as Biceps grabbed Kaz roughly and pushed him toward the door. I tried to follow, but Texas stepped between us.

"Where do you think you're taking them?" Texas demanded.

"What do you care? They'll be secure. Why don't you take care of rearming the controls?"

"Don't you tell me—"

"I'll tell you whatever I want," Biceps said. "I'm in command, remember?"

"I'll write you up."

"Stop, just stop it," Dr. Grace said, finally finding her voice. "Bickering's not going to help anything. We need to work together until Prentiss gets back—"

"I've got it under control, Genevieve," Biceps interrupted her coldly.

She glared at him, and I could tell she didn't care for being addressed by her first name. Or for being told what to do by these men, who, moments before, had told Kaz to kill her.

Tensions were high, and the haste with which Prentiss had assembled his team clearly hadn't helped. Only a few months had passed since Bryce's lab was destroyed, and Prentiss—with all his money and connections and resources— had rebuilt with astonishing speed. But some things could not be rushed, and unity was one of them. There were serious cracks in the organization. I wondered how we could take advantage of them.

Biceps forced Kaz to walk in front of him, and waved me along to join them. Texas stepped aside, but the glare he gave us was furious. "I'm writing this up," he repeated, and Biceps flipped him off as we walked single file toward the elevator.

"Look," Kaz said to Biceps when the elevator doors shut. "There's no reason for the gun. We're cooperating. If you just—"

"Shut it, Boy Scout," Biceps snapped.

Kaz shrugged, but he kept quiet.

"Move," Biceps ordered when the elevator doors opened onto the two-story atrium at the intersection of the building's wings. He led us toward the hall opposite the residential wing, but the scenery outside caught my attention. A flagstone patio led to the pond that had been on this land since before the park was built, though it didn't resemble the cattail-edged pond it had once been. It had been sculpted into an oval and planted with water lilies and overhanging willows. When I was a kid, the Morries used to fish there; now it was ringed by benches and picnic tables.

No one was enjoying the scenery now, though. In fact, there was no one in the hall besides us. Our footsteps echoed on the tiled floors, and I wondered if Prentiss was operating with fewer staff than had worked for Bryce. Had some of his team defected after the lab was destroyed? Or was it possible that they'd had second thoughts about the mission?

"I've got a little education in mind for you two," Biceps said, his voice dripping with sarcasm.

"We could just wait in our rooms," I suggested. "Until things are, you know . . . more stable."

"Yeah. You could. That's what Bonaventure would like, for us all to just sit around with our thumbs up our asses until Prentiss gets back here." Biceps scowled. "Only, I've got a better idea."

He stopped in front of a reinforced door. "The grand tour ends here."

He flipped up the top of a keypad and punched in a long series of digits before the door clicked open.

"Ladies first," he said, stepping aside with a flourish, and I stepped into the room.

It was all too familiar.

A choked gasp escaped my throat as I stumbled backward, but Biceps shoved me back in. I grabbed Kaz's arm, pressing against him while my heart stampeded.

The room was full of them. Half a dozen zombies sat in folding chairs, only their eyes moving when they saw us. I recoiled, remembering the terrifying experience of being attacked a few months earlier in Bryce's lab, when I'd accidentally stumbled on the room where he kept his specimens, a room very much like this one, right down to the folding chairs and the white T-shirts and khakis they wore.

I tried to turn away, but I found that I couldn't stop looking. They had all been young men. Four of them looked as though they had turned recently, their skin mostly intact, though pale and waxy. One of these four was very thin and had lost all its hair and looked like it had been sick for a long time. The other three had been injured; they had jagged scars on their faces and skulls, bruises from IVs and feeding tubes, limbs twisted and mangled and in one case missing, with a bandaged stump where the arm had been.

But the two who had turned less recently were even more horrifying. When a Healer heals a person at the moment of their death, they don't die, but they don't live, either. They enter an undead state, able to follow instructions but unable to communicate, no longer human, just functional shells that once held souls.

The undead are hard to kill. They can be burned to death, or drowned or beheaded or torn limb from limb, but anything else barely slows them down.

Eventually, though, the undead deteriorate, just as any corpse does, and expire. Prairie had told me it takes about three times as long as an ordinary dead body, but these two zombies looked like they were getting close: their flesh had swollen and ruptured, viscous fluids seeping into their clothes, dripping puddles on the floor. One of them was missing an eye, the cavern of the socket dripping pus, and its tongue was blackened and swelling and protruded from its mouth. The other had lost entire patches of flesh, and its bones and tendons were visible in its arms and its neck; a flap of skin hung from its jaw, revealing its gray shrunken gums and teeth in a skeletal leer.

"Like these guys?" Biceps demanded, his voice laced with amusement. "Some of our finest. Too bad these are all still test models. Working out a few of the final kinks and then we start production for real. Want to guess what just one of these babies goes for on the open market?"

"Who are you gonna sell to first?" Kaz demanded angrily. "Who's offering the most for suicide bombers these days?"

"Oh, that's right, you're the big patriot," Biceps said. "Lost your daddy in Iraq, and now you think it's your job to carry on in his shoes, is that it?"

I felt Kaz tense and I thought he was going to attack, but he forced himself back under control. "You don't have to love your country to believe people shouldn't blow each other up," he said through clenched teeth. "And doing it for money's evil."

Biceps laughed. "Pretty boy, you ain't going to hurt my feelings calling me names. I'm a capitalist, that's all. An opportunist. You must not have been paying attention in history class, because that's how this country got built—people taking advantage of their circumstances. You sit still, you get run over."

While I watched, a glistening trail of pinkish fluid leaked from the damaged skull of one of the more recent zombies, trailing down the side of its face and dripping onto its lap. It didn't blink, didn't flinch, but a wave of nausea passed through me.

"Here's a little something you ought to know about these fellas," Biceps said almost cheerfully. "They've been trained to respond only to certain voices. It's a new thing we're doing, so we can set it up so they follow only the buyer's orders. Bryce turned us on to it, actually."

"I thought Bryce was *dead*," I said.

Biceps chuckled. "Well, he wishes he was, anyway. Stay on track here, kids. This bunch won't listen to anybody but Prentiss and his top people. Which includes me. Whatever I tell them, they're gonna do, no questions asked. But you can holler at 'em all day long and it's like they won't even hear you. Got that?"

Of course I got that; I was a Healer. Didn't he understand that? The knowledge of what had been done to these poor men—boys, really, no doubt taken from battlefields overseas, where they could be conveniently "lost" by Prentiss's corrupt contacts in the services—weighed deep in my soul, because I too possessed the power to do this.

"Who did this?" I demanded. Somehow they'd found another Healer, but where? The Tarbells were the only ones left. Unless—

"You're not the only Healer around, little miss," Biceps smirked. "You should have been a little more careful when you sent your friend Zytka packing."

I couldn't breathe. I'd watched her wave goodbye. I'd watched her walk toward her gate at O'Hare, rolling her small suitcase behind her.

But I hadn't seen her get on the plane, hadn't seen it take off, hadn't talked to her after it landed.

Prentiss had gotten to her. I didn't know how, but I wasn't surprised. The more I knew about him, the more I feared him; he had connections and resources far beyond my comprehension. Somehow he'd kidnapped Zytka and forced her to make zombies for him, just as he'd forced her sisters—just as he meant to force me.

"Now you've managed to piss me off," Biceps continued. "So you're gonna chill here for tonight. Don't worry, if you follow instructions, you'll be just fine. Okay, boys." He addressed the zombies. "Our guests are going to stay in this box here, see?"

With the toe of his shoe, he traced a square on the floor, following the pattern of the tile. He pushed a few empty chairs out of the way to make the square about six feet across. "Now, if they stay in their box, you leave them alone, hear?"

The zombies stared at him, their eyes empty of emotion, but I knew they were absorbing his words.

"But if they step so much as an inch outside it, you tear 'em up. Kill them. Got it? Nod if you understand."

As if they were puppets joined by a single string, all six nodded, the decomposing ones' loose skin swaying gently.

"Now, I'd get on in there, if I was you," Biceps said, prodding me forward.

CHAPTER 28

KAZ AND I STOOD TOGETHER inside our imaginary prison, holding each other tightly.

"Boys, come stand around them, okay? Make like a ring-around-the-rosie."

The clatter of chairs being pushed back made me feel faint and I squeezed my eyes shut and pressed my face against Kaz's shirt and wished that I could just stay like that, pretending we were somewhere else, back in Chicago in the little neighborhood park, and that when I opened my eyes, I'd see tall buildings and cars going by and Kaz's gray eyes shining in the spring sun.

I forced myself to lift my head and look. The zombies shuffled slowly into a circle around us, their movements jerky and uncoordinated. The one who was missing an arm stumbled and fell—there was something very wrong with one of its legs—but it kept coming, crawling along the floor and dragging its damaged leg behind it. A terrible smell wafted from one of the rotting ones, and bits of crusted, scabbed flesh fell from it as it came closer.

They found their places, spaced evenly around our square, and stood staring at us with no expression at all, not menace or anger or craftiness—just nothing. But I knew that the minute we ventured past the boundary Biceps had drawn along the edge of the tiles, they would set on us like rabid dogs.

It had happened to me once before, and I would never forget the feel of their bony, cold fingers on my flesh, the sickening sponginess of their rotting bodies as I fought them.

"Prentiss isn't going to like this," Kaz said.

Uncertainty flashed briefly across Biceps's face, but he forced a laugh. I remembered the way he'd acted with the other guard—full of swagger, itching for a fight. He was a guy with something to prove. "Prentiss's got bigger things to worry about. Besides, as soon as he calls in, you can come out of there. This is just a little . . . activity to keep you busy."

And a chance for him to prove himself among the staff left behind, I thought.

"Ta-ta," Biceps said, giving us a limp little wave before letting himself out of the room.

We watched him go, but the zombies didn't. Their eyes stayed fixed on us.

When the door shut, I wrapped my arms even tighter around Kaz and forced myself to stay calm. I'd survived being afraid before.

I will get through this. I said the words in my mind, making myself believe them. I'd survived being shot at and hunted and kidnapped, and I would survive this, too.

"Piece of cake," I said shakily. "We just have to wait around a little while."

"Yeah," Kaz agreed, but I could tell he was worried. "Hailey, I think we should sit down and rest, but . . . we have to be careful."

That was an understatement. He was taller than the square was wide. And there would be no exceptions. All it would take was a hand or a foot—even a lock of my hair—crossing the lines and the zombies would be on us, going for blood.

They didn't know any other way.

We sat down gingerly, steering clear of the edges of our cell. Kaz sat cross-legged and I leaned back against him, his arms around me. That was when I realized that his hands were still bleeding from the broken glass.

"Let me," I said softly, and I held his hands in mine and lost myself in the healing. It was a good place to go; it calmed me and chased my fears away, if only for a moment. When I released Kaz's hands, there was no mark on them, and I knew that I had done well.

"That one looks like he's going to expire at any minute," Kaz said. The most decomposed zombie was barely standing, swaying on legs that were hardly able to hold up its rotting body. Its head lolled on its neck, and its empty socket stared, but it stayed in its spot.

For a moment, anyway. Then a convulsion shuddered through its body, and it collapsed.

Into our square.

It landed in a heap, body fluids spattering, flesh tearing loose from the bones, its crablike skeletal elbow inches away. I screamed and felt Kaz tightening his arms around me, forcing me to stay in place, but I fought him. I had to get away from it, and I wrestled against Kaz, trying to crawl away from the motionless thing, the seeping puddle in which it lay.

"Stop fighting me!" Kaz yelled into my ear, and I finally went slack against him. He was right. We had to stay in our square, even if it meant sharing it with the zombie. "Hailey, shut your eyes, just let me hold you, stop . . ."

He kept up like that, rocking me in his arms, whispering in my ear, for what felt like hours, until I finally stopped shaking. It took a long time. I kept my eyes closed, and Kaz talked, and I listened. He told me about his childhood, about the first time he'd had a vision. About missing his dad, about helping his mom in the salon. About his best friend, who moved to Kansas in middle school. About the first girl he kissed. About his dreams of learning to fly, of joining the air force.

I listened, and we rocked, and I tried to pretend we were back in the park. After a very long time, I felt a little better, and I told him about me. Things I had never told another soul. About wishing I had known my mother, wondering who my father was. About the imaginary friend I'd had who played with me in the woods behind the house.

We talked and talked until our voices were hoarse, the night passing slowly, and when there was a sound at the door, my eyes flew open and the sight of the zombies—still standing guard, motionless and ready—sent a fresh shock through me. I had almost managed to forget they were there.

Dr. Grace opened the door and her eyes widened.

"What the hell is going on!"

She shut the door behind her and leaned on it, her hand over her heart. "What on earth— Never mind. All of you— back off. Go sit in your chairs."

The zombies shuffled away from their posts around the square, back to their chairs—all except for the one next to us. A trickle of black fluid leaked from its mouth, and a fly buzzed around its crusted, ruined flesh.

"What happened?" Dr. Grace demanded.

"The guard—he told us to stay in here," Kaz said.

"In where?"

"This square." He traced the floor tiles to show her. "Or else he told them to, uh . . ."

I knew he didn't want to say it, so I said it for him: "To kill us."

Dr. Grace's expression hardened. "That's— Oh, for Pete's sake. There's little danger with the specimens, as long as everyone follows procedure. We aren't supposed to issue any orders at all that aren't clearly outlined on the test plan. All of you—stay where you are. You are to leave these two alone."

She directed the command at the zombies, but they gave no indication that they had heard.

"What about next time?" I demanded. "I mean, how many people can just walk in here and—and—tell them to do anything they want?"

Dr. Grace shook her head impatiently, a line etched between her eyebrows. "It's not like that. It's only the research team and security. And Prentiss, of course. Look, I'm not saying it's perfect, but this is all—I mean, nobody expected what happened today. Anyway, you're safe now. You can get up."

I stood and brushed grit off my clothes. I forced myself to back out of the square, holding Kaz's hand tightly.

"What about that one?" Kaz asked, pointing at the broken body on the floor. It was finally at peace, its rotting flesh no longer able to sustain life after death.

Dr. Grace sighed. "I'll call for cleanup. The tissues are sterile, if that's what you're worried about."

Kaz laughed shortly. "You think I'd worry about *that*? When I practically got ripped to shreds by those . . . things?"

"How can you stand it?" I asked. "How can you stand to work here, knowing what they're going to do with them?"

Dr. Grace blinked behind her glasses and frowned at me. "My area of expertise is precognition and psychokinesis," she said, hedging. "I'm head of psychic research, but my contact with the . . . specimens . . . is really quite limited. I work with our psychic subjects, who are, I assure you, all very much alive."

"So as long as you get to study whatever it is you want to study, that makes all of this"—I gestured at the rows of zombies—"okay?"

"I'd like to secure the lab now," Dr. Grace said before turning away from me and muttering an order into a small handheld device.

"Answer her question," Kaz said. "We deserve to know."

Dr. Grace frowned, considering. Finally she gave us a brisk nod. "I don't think you want to be here when the cleanup team's working, so let's go. We can talk on the way."

CHAPTER 29

DR. GRACE KEPT UP a fast pace through the halls. It was early morning, the sun streaming through windows set high in the walls. We hadn't slept at all, and it was a struggle to keep up with her.

"You don't understand how hard it is to find funding for what most people consider a pseudoscience," she said. "You, of all people, should be sympathetic to that, Hailey."

"Me?" I demanded. "Why?"

"Because you yourself have a gift that society doesn't understand. How many people would believe you if you went out into the world and announced you were a Healer?" There was a bitter edge to her voice that told me she was speaking from experience. "Even when you can prove—when you have *evidence* of—naturally occurring psychic phenomena, the scientific community is so inbred and resistant—"

She paused and bit her lip in frustration. "I've known since I started my doctoral thesis that precognition is real, and I could back it up. But when I left the university, do you know how many job offers I had? *Zero.* No one would touch me with a ten-foot pole."

"So . . . let me guess. When you met Prentiss, he was your dream come true. Right?"

Dr. Grace glanced at me suspiciously. "If you are implying—"

"I'm not implying anything," I said. "I'm just saying that if he was the only guy around willing to pay you to do the work you wanted, I guess that made it awfully hard to be judgmental when he told you that they were breeding zombies in here. Only, I can't help thinking that even then, you would have a problem with what they do with the zombies, who they're selling them to."

She gave me a patronizing look. "Hailey, just because something's illegal doesn't make it immoral or unnecessary. The specimens are used in settings where it's simply too dangerous to send a living human, like when they have to do repairs on an oil rig or defuse explosives, things like that—"

"What?" I demanded. "Is *that* what they told you?"

"Prentiss's selling them to foreign militaries," Kaz added. "For war applications."

Dr. Grace's face darkened. "Don't be ridiculous. Just because Prentiss's background is military doesn't mean . . ."

But she didn't finish her sentence. I could see her thinking it through, coming to the inevitable conclusion that she'd been lied to.

"There's no time for this," she finally sputtered. "Look, if you do as I say, I'll let you talk to the boy."

"You'll let us see Chub?" I asked, the zombies temporarily forgotten. "Now?"

"Yes, but there is one condition—you must tell him to cooperate with me."

"Cooperate . . . how?" I was immediately suspicious.

She waved her hand impatiently. "Nothing you need to worry about, nothing that will harm him. Just simple tests."

"What kind of tests?"

She sighed and walked faster. "Chub shows remarkable psychic ability. My work here is to find ways to identify high psychics more readily, and train them to exercise greater control over their skills. He is a perfect subject, but he's been . . . reluctant."

I wondered if Dr. Grace knew about the Banished, the Seers. What exactly had Prentiss told his staff after the first lab had been destroyed? It was coming together in my mind: as long as his employees didn't understand the applications for the work they were doing, they weren't likely to balk at helping him build his war machines.

It was how Bryce had convinced Prairie to work for him, telling her that their work would benefit people, then used her for her talents.

"I'll tell him to cooperate," I said.

"Good. Because he's been remarkably resistant, almost selectively mute. I can count on two hands the number of words he's spoken since arriving here."

Arriving—as though he'd come some other way than having been kidnapped and thrown in the back of a car. I bit back a sharp retort.

Dr. Grace stopped in front of an unremarkable door, opening it with a key from her pocket.

Chub was kneeling on the floor of a small carpeted room, playing with a toy made from stiff colored wire strung with beads. He looked up, frowning with concentration, at the sound of the door.

And then he burst into a smile that nearly broke my heart.

"Hayee! Kaz!" he shouted, and raced over to us, wrapping his arms around my legs, the way he had since he'd first come to live with us two years earlier. After giving me a noisy kiss, he went for Kaz, who pretended to stumble backward from the impact, making Chub squeal with laughter. Kaz picked him up and swung him in a circle before handing him gently to me, and I took him in my arms and hugged him hard, tears in my eyes.

"I've missed you," I whispered. I set him down but kept my body between him and Dr. Grace, holding his hand tightly.

Chub's room was a smaller version of mine, with the same subtly colored walls, the soft drapes, the bathroom off to the side. There were bookshelves filled with board books and toys, a bed, a dresser. A mobile of planets hung out of reach from the ceiling. A rocking horse stood in the corner.

There was one big difference, though. Whereas my room had a broad window with a view of the fields stretching out into the distance, Chub's window was fake. I could see the painted wall between the slats of the blinds that filled the false frame.

Kaz had noticed too. He went to the wall and jerked the blinds' cord, pulling them up to reveal the square of wall underneath. "You couldn't even let the poor kid see the sun?"

Dr. Grace shrugged. "We are keeping distractions to a minimum during the testing."

"You mean, because he wouldn't talk to you," I said accusingly. "You're punishing him."

"Not so. All of our subjects in the psychic evaluation program are kept in a distraction-free environment."

"Who else have you got?" I asked. But I knew something that she didn't—the "subjects" Prentiss meant to bring into the lab would all be Banished. That was why he'd contacted Rattler. It was what they had been arguing about on the phone the day before. Prentiss probably figured he could convince Seers to cooperate with or without Rattler—but he had enough doubt that he'd been trying hard to force Rattler to be his middleman.

And that was why Prentiss had taken Prairie.

Which meant that he knew how Rattler felt about Prairie. I had to hand it to Prentiss—his intelligence was remarkable.

Dr. Grace shrugged. "There are other subjects who I've studied at length," she said.

"In Chicago?"

"That's not something we need to discuss. Now, I suggest you make the most of your time together." She looked at her watch. "You have fifteen minutes."

Fifteen minutes, I thought with a sinking heart. Not a lot of time. "Can you at least leave us alone?"

Dr. Grace shook her head. "I'm afraid not, but I'll stay out of the way. You won't even notice me."

But it was hard not to notice the way she watched us, sitting in a straight-backed chair in the corner. I turned my back on her, but I could still feel her eyes on me.

The fifteen minutes passed more quickly than I'd imagined possible. Kaz and Chub rolled on the floor in a tickle fight; Chub crawled into my lap and pretended to read a book about birds, pointing at each page and telling me what he saw. "This a red bird. It has a worm, see?"

I was proud of my little adopted brother; he'd continued to learn and develop even here. His preschool teachers in Chicago had told Prairie during his first week that he was catching up with the other kids; as I held him and listened to him chatter, I was so full of hope for his future that I thought my heart would burst. He chattered on about ducks and monsters and numbers, about games he had played with Dr. Grace. He told me about playing hide-and-seek with numbers, and good monsters and bad monsters, and I was relieved that being cooped up in the room hadn't dampened his spirits or taken his imagination away.

"Time's up," Dr. Grace said, rising from her chair. "Chub, tell Hailey and Kaz goodbye. You did very well today. If you can talk to me the way you talk to them, tomorrow when we do our games together, maybe you can see them again."

Chub pressed against me, holding on to my arm with his hands. "I don't like her games," he mumbled.

Dr. Grace blinked. "They're fun," she said unconvincingly.

Prairie was a scientist too, but she was nothing like Dr. Grace; she was lively and intuitive and interested in the world around her. And she loved me, of that I was certain; watching Dr. Grace, I wasn't convinced that she loved anyone or anything other than her work.

She was a zealot. That was the key that Prentiss had figured out. Zealots were devoted, but they were also dangerous: because they were so focused on a single passion, they ignored everything else, allowing terrible things to happen.

In her own way, Dr. Grace was as dangerous as Prentiss.

I glanced around the room, looking for a camera; there it was, up in the corner over the door. I caught Kaz's eye and he gave me a tiny nod to show he'd seen it. But what could we do? I'd be surprised if someone wasn't monitoring Chub at all times. And the rest of us too, for that matter; somewhere there was undoubtedly a bank of monitors showing all the rooms, including mine and Kaz's. There was no way we would be able to make a move without being observed.

At least I had seen for myself that Chub was all right.

Dr. Grace led us back into the hall. My last glimpse of Chub was of him standing in the middle of the room, watching us without blinking, a sad pout on his face. It nearly broke my heart.

"I can't wait until tomorrow to see him again," I said. "Let me stay with him. I can sleep on the floor."

Dr. Grace shook her head. "That is not possible."

I felt my frustration escalate. I was tired, to the point of breaking. "Who the hell are you to say what's possible? You let Prentiss order you around, you let him tell you what to study and how, and you think you're really doing the work you were trained to do?"

"Now wait just—"

"My aunt was just like you," I continued. "She believed Bryce. She did everything he told her to. Right up until the day he tried to have her killed. You saw how they were downstairs, how they were ready to let *us* kill you. Is that really what you want?"

"Prentiss doesn't—"

"Prentiss only cares about one thing," Kaz interrupted. "And it's not you. Look, we'll help you with your research, we'll get Chub to cooperate with you, but you have to do something for us."

"Like what?"

"Let Hailey stay in the room with Chub." Kaz looked at me as he said it, his gray eyes gentle. He knew how badly I needed to be with Chub.

"I can't do that," Dr. Grace protested. "There's a video feed. There's no way I could get away with it. There's someone watching the monitor twenty-four hours . . ."

Then she paused, looking thoughtful.

"What?" I demanded.

"There *is* something. A small favor that I can do for you. But only if you promise that *you'll* do everything you can to help me with Chub."

Kaz and I exchanged looks. "Depends on what it is."

Dr. Grace gave him a small smile. "I can let you see your mother."

"She's *here*?" Kaz demanded. My heart sank—had they kidnapped her, too?

She shook her head. "No, but they've put surveillance cameras in your house." She looked embarrassed and didn't meet Kaz's eye. "I can take you to the viewing room and you can watch the live feed. You'll be able to see her on-screen, real time. The resolution is quite good."

Kaz and I looked at each other, and I could see that he was trying to contain his fury. But it was nothing that we hadn't expected; we both knew they would be keeping close tabs on Anna.

"All right," he said quietly. It was the best deal we were going to get, and we both knew it. "But how can you justify bringing us there? Won't Prentiss mind?"

Dr. Grace shrugged dismissively. "Prentiss isn't here. And besides, I outrank everyone in security."

So it all came down to her position within the organization,

I thought as we followed her back toward the center of the complex. She was intimidated by Prentiss, and there was little trust among her and the other senior staff—but she didn't care about those whose rank was below hers.

That was the arrogance that had contributed to Bryce's downfall, the belief in ruling with intimidation. He had thought that as long as he was in charge, he was invulnerable. Dr. Grace was making the same dangerous mistake, and I wondered how we could use it against her.

CHAPTER 30

SHE LED US TO THE TOWER that anchored the main building, rising above the rest of the office park. I had thought it was decorative, and in fact the top of it probably was, with its tall arched windows. But there was a floor below that I hadn't noticed from outside, and that was where Dr. Grace took us.

The room was octagonal, windowless and ringed with large monitors. As Dr. Grace had promised, the resolution was remarkable. At first glance I saw the cafeteria, empty now except for a lone custodian moving the tables out of the way to vacuum, displayed on a four-foot-wide screen, and the courtyard out front, where a gardener in coveralls tended a row of small trees. Four people wearing headsets were seated at workstations, watching the dozen monitors, making notes on their laptops. They glanced up as Dr. Grace walked in, and one of them moved his earpiece out of the way and looked at her questioningly.

"It's all right, Chetan," she said. "They're here to observe with me."

The man shrugged and adjusted his earpiece.

There was an empty area in the middle of the room, behind the bank of workstations, and Dr. Grace led us there. We had an unobstructed view over the heads of the other viewers. "You have five minutes," she whispered. "Look at the screen over there."

I spotted Anna immediately. She was standing at a window of her bedroom, already dressed for work in her nursing scrubs. She had her back to the camera, her long, wavy chestnut hair pulled into a low ponytail, her sharp-angled shoulders sloped in defeat. Next to me, Kaz sucked in his breath.

"She's all right," I said softly.

"She doesn't know that I am, though," he muttered. "That must be killing her. . . ."

Almost as though she could hear us speaking, Anna turned away from the window and regarded the rest of her room bleakly. The bed was neatly made, a stack of folded laundry waiting to be put away.

She touched the edge of the bed, smoothing out the spread, and then she slowly lowered herself to the floor. For a moment I thought she had collapsed, but when she folded her hands together under her chin, I realized she had knelt to pray.

Kaz squeezed my hand, and my heart constricted with

pain for him. I had seen Kaz fearless in the face of incredible odds, even death—but watching his mother struggle seemed like more than he could bear.

I turned away to give him privacy. Dr. Grace was conferring quietly with one of the technicians, going over something he was showing her on a log sheet. I looked at the other banks of monitors, which displayed every corner of the facility. There were bedrooms like Chub's, but with real windows and more personal details—staff quarters, I assumed. There were views of the parking garage, the courtyard, the research facilities. Some were empty, and in others people worked at computers and banks of equipment.

There was the specimen room; I saw that the zombies were lined up in their chairs, where we'd left them. The one that had nearly fallen on us had been removed, but there was a stain on the floor where it had lain. I glanced quickly away from that screen.

There was a hospital bed with a lumpy, still form under a white sheet. Another zombie? But something wasn't right. . . .

It took me a moment to absorb what I was seeing.

Sensors blinked and tubes protruded from the body's throat and extremities. As I watched, the body shifted slightly, its arm skittering a few inches on the sheet. Clawed fingers scrabbled at nothing. But what was wrong with them? They were hideously deformed, mere stumps, crusted with . . .

What was that?

I squinted at the face exposed at the head of the bed and felt my stomach turn. The skin had melted from the bone, a mask of peeling, bandaged shreds attached to a skull. A lip-less mouth pulled back from leering teeth. Its eyes stared piteously at the ceiling, its lashes and eyebrows gone. There was no hair on its skull, and its ears were mere knobs of flesh—

And that was when I knew: this tortured body had been horribly burned, and then saved by extraordinary measures, the best medical care money could buy. It would have been far kinder to let it die; its every moment was screaming tor-ture, but its lungs had been too badly damaged to produce a scream.

It was Bryce Safian.

The man we had left for dead. The man who'd been pulled from the inferno of his laboratory, carried out on a stretcher, one charred foot dangling free. From what I could see, most of his body had been burned beyond recognition.

But Prentiss had contacts everywhere, sources I could only imagine. If there was a way, he would buy or steal it. He would pay people to perform miracles on Bryce, and pay oth-ers to look the other way.

In the old lab, the one we had destroyed, Bryce had been in charge, and I had feared him. He tried to imprison me, to use me and Prairie to learn how to turn ordinary people into Healers. Had he succeeded, he could have produced the seeds of World War III, giving every army that could afford to pay access to zombies who would carry out their acts of war.

We had destroyed Bryce's lab, his data—but we hadn't de-stroyed his backups. We didn't think it mattered: with him dead, the passwords and locations were lost forever. But with him alive . . .

That was why he was here. Even if all he could do was scrawl on a pad of paper—even if all he could do was blink yes or no—with enough patience and enough time, they could make him tell everything. First would be the passwords; then they would force him to explain the data. By keeping him alive, they had round-the-clock access to a consultant whose every moment was clearly agony.

My heart sank. If they had already got the passwords from him, everything was lost. There was no way we would be able to pull off burning down a lab a second time. I had no doubt they'd redoubled the security here. They would be on high alert for any kind of invasion.

But . . .

Bryce was still alive, and there had to be a reason. As much as I hated Prentiss, I didn't believe he was deliberately cruel. Bryce held the key to the work being done here.

So we had to get to Bryce.

I glanced at Dr. Grace again, but she was engrossed in the report she was reading, tracing a column of numbers with her fingernail. Next to me Kaz watched his mother pray and held my hand tightly in his.

After a moment Dr. Grace summoned us. "Time's up, I'm afraid," she said. "We need to get you two to your rooms so you can get some rest. If you'll follow me?"

As he turned to go, Kaz traced a fleeting sign of the cross on his forehead, chest and shoulders and mouthed the words

I love you to his mother. She continued to pray, her lips moving steadily, her back straight.

As we left the lab, I—who had never set foot in a church—said the most desperate prayer of my life.

Keep us safe, and help us do what must be done.

CHAPTER 31

THE BROWN-GLASSES LADY brought her toys and she put a duck behind the hiding thing. Chub knew it was a duck because she left the top off the box when she came in and the duck was at the top of the box and when she put something behind the hiding thing the duck was not on the top of the box. Chub had a duck like that. Prairie gave it to him and it went in his tub when he had a bath and when he didn't have a bath it went in the blue basket so Hailey could take her bath. Hailey did not have a duck and she didn't play with his duck either when she took her bath.

Chub wanted the duck that the lady brought, except it wouldn't be the same as his duck. It looked the same but it wouldn't be the same. Nothing was the same here and he wanted to go home. Hailey came yesterday and Kaz came yesterday, but it wasn't time to go home yet. They could only play with him a little while. Hailey was sad when they had to go. She didn't want to go and Kaz didn't want to go. The brown-glasses lady made them leave and he wished the lady would leave, but she came back.

The lady pretended she was very smart but she wasn't very smart. Because the bagel, she said if Chub didn't eat the bagel she would have to take the bagel away. But Chub put the bagel in his pocket. The pants today had a pocket and he put the bagel in the pocket and the lady didn't know he put the bagel there. The pants were red. His shirt had a bug on it. A bug picture. Chub was waiting to see if he liked the bug or not. He put his hand on the bug picture a lot. It was shiny.

"So, Chub, can you tell me what is behind the screen?"

Ask ask ask. The lady asked questions and asked. Chub had to let some words out today because he told Hailey he would. He said words, he said *no* and *dog* and *thank you* because everyone likes when you say thank you. The lady liked it when he said *thank you* but then her mouth was mad again.

"Is it . . . the dog? Or maybe the shovel? Or the cup?"

Chub looked at her mouth making words. It was not the dog. It was not the shovel. Or the cup. It was the duck. She knew the duck was behind the hiding thing. She wanted him to say duck.

"Duck."

The brown-glasses lady jumped up fast and Chub thought she might climb over the hiding thing but then she sat down on her chair again. The lady looked happy and Chub made a smile for her, because Hailey said to *help the nice lady* but Chub was thinking about Prairie because Prairie was in his mind-picture this morning and Prairie looked sad and the eye man was there and he put his hand on Prairie's face and she looked sad. The eye man used to come visit Gram and he was scary and Hailey pushed a stick in his eye and made it crazy. Hailey pushed that stick in his eye but now he put his hand on Prairie's face and then he put his face on her face and Chub wanted to tell Prairie to *skedaddle,* but it was only a mind-picture and he couldn't tell her anything.

"That's right, it *is* a duck, Chub! Aren't you a smart boy! Aren't you a *good* boy!"

Chub was a smart boy and he was a good boy but he wished the lady would close her mouth and he wished Hailey and Kaz would come back and he wished the eye man would leave Prairie alone.

CHAPTER 32

IT WAS NOT DR. GRACE who came to my room at dinnertime, but a tall bald man in white scrubs that barely covered the holster on his belt. I asked him if Prentiss had returned yet, and I could tell by the way he avoided the question that he hadn't.

That made me feel a little better, because I knew it meant they hadn't caught up with Prairie yet. Even if she was with Rattler, I felt like her odds were better than if she ended up here, trapped with the rest of us.

When we arrived in the dining room, I was relieved to see Kaz sitting alone with a full plate of food in front of him, pushing pasta around with a fork.

"Can I sit with him?" I asked.

"You can sit anywhere you want," my escort said. "Dr.

Grace will be here for you sometime in the next half hour, so eat up."

I went through the line quickly, taking the first things I saw and piling them on a tray. When Kaz saw me sliding into the chair across from him, some of the tension eased from his face.

"You look . . . tired," I said. His skin was pale and he had dark circles under his eyes. I had slept fitfully after Dr. Grace escorted us back to our rooms, my thoughts swirling and nagging at me. It looked like Kaz hadn't fared any better.

He covered my hand with his own, his touch warm and enveloping.

"I had a vision, Hailey."

I wanted to tell him about Bryce—about what I'd seen on the monitor, about what it meant—but that would have to wait.

"What did you see?"

"I don't know," he said, crumpling a napkin in his fist, clearly frustrated. "I've been sitting here trying to figure it out."

"Describe it step by step," I suggested. "Maybe with both of us . . ."

Kaz rubbed his forehead in frustration, pushing back the hair that always fell in his eyes. "It was Bryce. He was . . . disappearing. I don't know how to describe it. It was like he was fading away from the bottom up. He didn't have any hair, but there wasn't a scratch on him. I swear, though—I swear it was him."

My heart thrummed with excitement and fear. "That's because he's alive."

"What!"

I explained what I'd seen earlier on the monitors. The body in the bed, the machines keeping him alive. His burnt-off fingers and ears, the lips that had melted away from his gums.

"They saved him somehow, Kaz," I concluded. "I don't know how. And I don't know how long he can survive in that condition. But he's here."

"But in the vision—Hailey, he wasn't burned. I don't know . . . maybe, I mean, what if the vision was really from the past, you know?"

"That doesn't make sense. Your visions are never about the past."

"But there's no other way to—"

"No. You saw that vision," I interrupted, suddenly sure of what it meant. "That's because he gets healed. It has to be."

Kaz slowly closed his mouth, and I could see him putting it all together. "So we have to find a way to stop them. They must be planning to use the Healer they have here and—"

"I don't think so," I said. "I think it's *me* who heals him."

"You! But why? Why would you—"

"I'm not sure," I admitted. "But it's me. I . . . just know it."

What I didn't say was that ever since I'd seen Bryce on the

monitors, I had felt it stirring inside, the desire—the need—to heal. The words were a whispered chorus under my thoughts, and my fingers tingled and twitched with the longing to touch his ravaged body.

"But if you heal him, Prentiss'll have everything he needs to re-create the lab, and—"

"No, I think I need to heal him so that he can help us *destroy* the backups," I said. "Did you see anything that would help us find where in the complex they're keeping him? Or how we might be able to bust him out?"

Kaz was silent for a moment, concentrating. "I don't know. I mean, it was just Bryce, and he was fading away. He had . . . like, this expression, sort of . . . manic, you know? Kind of crazed. What about what you saw on the monitor? Anything about the room that would tell you where it was?"

I closed my eyes and concentrated, remembering. All that equipment . . . the wires and tubes snaking from his destroyed body, the screens blipping and blinking. But most of all I remembered the pure agony on what was left of his face.

"Nothing," I whispered.

"It's okay. . . . I might have an idea. Remember when we went to Bryce's lab? You went first, to create a distraction?"

"Yeah, and then you and Prairie took off down the hall and—"

"Yeah, but before that. The guard. What was his name? . . . Maynard."

"Maynard," I repeated, remembering.

He had been a heavyset guy in his late fifties, sitting

behind a desk, sleepily reading a newspaper. I'd pretended to be upset, told him there'd been an accident, begged him to come outside and see—so Kaz and Prairie could sneak past him into the lab—but he wouldn't listen. He had wanted to make some calls. I remembered his soft-palmed hand reaching for the phone, remembered my panic as I'd seen our entire scheme going down the drain, and then I'd reached across the desk, almost without thinking, and my hand had settled on the soft warm skin of his neck and I'd—

"I remember."

"Good. Because you have to do it one more time."

He looked troubled, his eyes avoiding my gaze. I knew there was something he wasn't telling me.

"What is it?" I asked. "Tell me. I need to know. I can't do this unless I know everything."

"There was . . . That wasn't the only vision I had."

My throat went dry with fear. The vision of Bryce had been bad enough. What more could he have seen? "What was it?"

"Well, it was a place. A little neighborhood in the middle of nowhere, full of run-down houses. There were two streets that crossed in the middle of the neighborhood; there were dogs lying in the street, kids fighting over nothing. Old cars up on blocks, boarded-up windows."

"That's Trashtown," I murmured.

"Rattler was there. And he had Prairie with him."

CHAPTER 33

RATTLER HUNG HIS HEAD with shame, because the worn old dress was no thing worthy of Prairie. But with all her pretty new clothes burned up at the Pollitt house, this dress was all he had to offer, his dead mama's Sunday dress that she wore until she quit getting dressed at all. He should have got shut of it. Should have burnt up all his mama's things when she died. Instead he'd scrubbed the house down to raw wood— floors, walls, ceilings—he'd scrubbed away the coughing and moaning of her last months and he'd scrubbed away the memories of her face swoll up from his daddy's fist and he'd scrubbed away every long-ago morning she turned him out to run wild through Trashtown so she could take her cure.

The box of her things stayed sealed up neat in the closet upstairs. Rattler would drive it to the dump. He would get new clothes for Prairie; her new clothes would hang in the closet just so. Prairie would do woman things to the house, curtains and fancy soap and such. That was not a job for Rattler, but he'd scrubbed until the skin rubbed off his knuckles and he'd split and stacked the wood and beat the rugs and caned the chairs and rubbed the dust from the lamps.

The shirt Prairie wore was too hot for June and she didn't have nothing else with her. Prairie had come to him with nothing and that was as it should be. Before long, Prairie would shed the city like a king snake sheds its skin; her hair would get long and her green eyes would grow bright again for him.

"Put it on, girl," Rattler said roughly, holding the worn dress out to her. He hated to see her standing so straight and still in his kitchen in the warm evening, sweat on her brow, her shirt buttoned up to her neck. He would buy a fan. He would buy a fan for every window. "Ain't much but it'll keep you cool. We'll go to town soon and git you things."

"I don't need anything," she said, not looking at him. Crazy talk. This was her home now; she should be looking at her new cups and plates and her new silver chest that had been his mama's. She should be thinking where did she want the chairs, the dish drainer, the broom. She didn't look at any of her new things. Didn't notice the flowers in the jar on the table, the cloth from so long ago Rattler didn't know who had stitched it, which he took out of the hutch just for her.

Rattler sighed and bunched the old dress in his fist. He would throw out his mother's things. He would pour Prairie a glass of water. He would tell her to fetch him a shined apple, rub his knotted-up shoulders, sing him one of the old songs. He would make her sit down. He would make her mind him. He would see himself in her wide green eyes.

Rattler looked at Prairie and he didn't know what to do.

CHAPTER 34

SO HE HAD TAKEN HER HOME.

I sat without speaking, thinking about it. I shouldn't have been surprised. Now that Derek's family farm had been blown sky-high, Rattler had nowhere else to take her. It was hard to imagine that his house, the house he had grown up in, which had been his father's before him, was much worse than the abandoned farmhouse—but I knew enough about Trashtown to know that it could be a lot worse.

"He won't like that," I said. "That's going to make him all the more determined to sell the Seers out to Prentiss, so he can afford something nicer for Prairie."

"He really . . . loves her?"

I frowned. "I guess you could say that. I mean, if you can call that love."

"No, I only meant that if she asked him to help us get Chub out, maybe he'd do it."

"Get *Rattler* to help us? After he tried to lock us up?"

"It's just a thought, Hailey. We're sort of running out of options here."

"Yeah, but—"

Before I could finish the thought, Dr. Grace appeared, checking her watch and holding a sheaf of papers bound by a large clip. "All right, you two," she said with forced cheer. "We have a couple of hours before we're done for the night, and I'd like to use it with you, Kaz. Hailey, you can come along if you like. Who knows, maybe you'll come in handy."

"You want to start testing me before Prentiss gets back," Kaz said.

Dr. Grace blinked. "That's not—"

"Did they find Prairie?" I demanded.

She pressed her lips together and didn't answer. "Leave your trays. Someone will clean up. Let's go."

"Just answer that one question, and we won't give you any trouble," I said. "Come on, it doesn't make a difference. I'll find out eventually anyway."

She hesitated, rubbing her temples. "They reported in, and they'll be back very soon. I'm sure they will find her soon. And her abductor."

"'Abductor'?" Kaz demanded incredulously. "Seriously? Uh, isn't that incredibly hypocritical, since you people kidnapped her first?"

"Look," Dr. Grace said angrily. "I am tired of being forced to defend things that are outside of my purview. I don't know what is going on up there and I don't really want to. I have a job to do and I would like to get started, so if you'll kindly—"

"There's a reason you want to start now, before they get back," Kaz said as he and I followed her out of the dining room. Everyone else had finished eating, and the dining room was empty. "You're afraid that Prentiss won't let you. Why is that, Dr. Grace?"

"Nothing could be further from the truth," Dr. Grace snapped in a brittle tone that implied he'd come very close to the truth.

My guess was that she had spent the last several hours thinking about what we had told her. About what the zombies were really going to be used for. Maybe she was having a moral crisis, wondering if she could continue working for a man who committed such atrocities. I wanted to believe that.

And maybe, knowing that she wouldn't be working here much longer, she wanted to spend as much time as possible with her most promising subjects: Chub, and now Kaz.

As we started up the ornate curving stairs to the upper floor, Kaz touched my arm, and I fell back with him. He silently pointed to the stairs that curved above us, and mouthed the word *now*.

As we neared the landing between floors, Kaz tackled Dr. Grace around the waist. Her feet swung off the floor and she made an "oof" sound as the air was knocked out of her.

"Do it, Hailey," Kaz whispered. Before Dr. Grace could recover enough to scream, I put my hand to her neck, closed my eyes and felt the swirling dark sensation as my blood rushed and roiled, and then she went limp.

I'd done it—the same thing I had done to the security guard. I hadn't injured her; I'd just put her into a deep sleep, my touch acting like a powerful magnet that temporarily blunted her conscious mind.

"What now?" I demanded. "They're going to—"

"Get her keys. Fast."

He held her under the armpits and started dragging her across the landing toward a door I'd missed earlier, a plain flat door set into the stretch of wall behind the curving staircase. I scrambled through her pockets for the ring of keys I'd seen her use earlier. I found it and then on an impulse reached for the holster attached to her belt and took her gun, too, surprised at its weight in my hand.

"Jackpot," I whispered as I slipped the gun into my pocket and jammed one of the two keys on the heavy silver ring into the lock. It worked. I guessed it was a master key, one that would open many different rooms in the complex. One of the perks of seniority.

Kaz shouldered the door open and I slipped into the darkness behind him and pulled the door shut, plunging us into total darkness. My knees struck something sharp and hard and I went down, landing on a cold floor.

Then I was still—as still as I could be—listening to the metallic echo of my impact, and our breathing. After what

217

seemed like a long time, Kaz whispered, "I'm going to set her down, okay?"

"Where are we?"

"Janitor's closet, I think. I noticed it at lunch, the way the stairway curves. They have cameras at the bottom and the top, but they missed this one spot."

I reached blindly for the object I'd tripped on, and felt the shape of a wheeled mop bucket. I backed up on my hands and knees until I found the wall behind me. I leaned back against brooms hanging from hooks, pulling my knees up to my chest. I waited for my eyes to adjust to the darkness, but there was no light, not even a slim crack coming from under the door.

"I'm going to wake her up," I whispered.

"What? She could make all kinds of noise in here—"

"I got her gun, right?"

"Yes, but—"

"She knows we won't kill her, since we didn't when we had the chance. But she doesn't know how badly we're willing to hurt her. Let's take advantage of her doubts."

I was pretending a bravery I didn't feel. If we were caught, our few tiny freedoms would be taken away. I'd be a prisoner in my cell twenty-four hours a day. There would be no more visits with Chub. No chances for Kaz to see his mom. And I'd never know if Prairie was safe—unless they found her, in which case they'd drag her here to be a prisoner, like the rest of us.

"Now let's make her take us to Bryce," I said.

"I thought you'd want to get Chub."

"Kaz, we can't. Not yet. We can't go for him until we're ready. Until we're sure." As much as I longed to free Chub right away, he would only slow us down.

And if there was a chance to end this for good, it lay with Bryce. I longed to see Chub, to hug him and kiss his soft downy cheeks, but we had to fix this first.

Or die trying.

The thought flashed through my mind before I could stop it. We were at a point of no return, having taken a hostage. In the past the staff hadn't shot to kill, because we were too valuable. They might still spare my life, because my healing gift was too rare for them to risk losing. But Kaz . . . no one knew the extent of his gift but me. There was no reason for the guards to let him live if we got into a firefight.

"This has to work," I whispered as I reached for Kaz. We squeezed each other's hands in the dark, and then he guided my fingers to Dr. Grace's neck and pressed them against her skin.

The thing I did, when I closed my eyes and emptied my mind, was the opposite of what I'd done before. The swirl was the same, the rushing blood, the voices, but I reversed the power of my touch, willed the stilled soul of Dr. Grace to awaken.

I felt her stir and then struggle to sit up.

"Where—what—"

I fumbled for the gun in my pocket. It was a good fit, heavy and smooth and warm from my body. I pressed the barrel against Dr. Grace's neck, careful not to touch the trigger. I would not—could not—shoot her.

"This is your gun," I whispered. "You are here with me and Kaz and in a moment we are going to open the door and you are going to take us to see Bryce."

"Who?" Dr. Grace asked, and I realized she was thinking fast.

"Nice try, but I know you know who I mean," I said. "Bryce Safian. I know he's here. I saw him on the monitors."

"I don't—"

I jabbed a little harder against her neck with the barrel of the gun. "I don't have a lot of patience right now."

"Make it look natural," Kaz said. "Lead us directly to him. Don't stop and don't talk to anyone. I'll keep the gun hidden, but I won't hesitate to shoot you this time."

"Don't be stupid," Dr. Grace said. "If you shoot me, you'll be dead in minutes."

"I don't think so," I said. "I'm way too valuable to them."

"And I'm a damn good shot," Kaz said. Another lie, but he made it sound plausible. "I'll take out as many as I can before I go down. Who knows? We might even get to the exit. You willing to take that chance?"

There was a silence while we waited for Dr. Grace to think it through.

"I'll open the door now," I said. "Remember, straight to Safian. If it makes you feel better, think about the fact that if we succeed, you'll be free to go find some nice legitimate lab somewhere and do your little experiments in peace."

220

And then I took a deep breath and felt for the doorknob, and we stood blinking in the bright sun. There was no one in sight. I handed the gun to Kaz and gave Dr. Grace a gentle shove.

The walk to Bryce's room was uneventful. A couple of people passed us, but one was talking angrily into his phone and the other was so distracted by a printout he was carrying that he barely acknowledged us.

The longer Prentiss was gone, the more the place was falling apart.

When Dr. Grace stopped in front of a door and reached for her keys, she came up with nothing. I palmed her keys from my own pocket, resisting the urge to gloat.

But when I opened the door, one glance inside the room wiped the smirk off my face.

Chapter 35

Kaz herded us inside and pushed the door closed behind us, then took my arm and pulled me close.

I pressed my face against his chest, not wanting to go any closer to the thing in the bed. It was like the scene on the monitor, only real. In person, Bryce's body was even more horrifying, the scabbed flesh red and black, his face a nightmare of agony.

After a moment I regained my composure and forced myself to step closer. "Can you see us?" I asked, my voice shaking.

Bryce's eyes rolled in his head, but then they focused on me.

"Do you know who we are?" I asked, swallowing my revulsion and forcing myself to approach the edge of the bed. I was close enough that if I wanted to, I could touch his ruined skin. Instead I worked hard to focus my gaze on his eyes.

"Hehh . . . ," he said, a terrible, rasping moan issuing from deep in his throat. "Heeehhhlie."

Hailey.

"That's right. And Kaz is here too. And Dr. Grace."

He looked at them, moving his head only the tiniest bit, his body racked with painful convulsions by the effort.

Suddenly the hatred I had stored up against him withered, and I felt only pity.

"Mr. Safian, can you help us destroy the data?"

He stared at me with a question in his eyes, a need, a hunger, and as much as I longed to shrink away from him, into Kaz's strong arms, I forced myself to stay where I was.

"Yehhhh . . . ihhh you kihhhh eee."

I glanced at Kaz, unable to understand Bryce's words. His lips had split and peeled and burnt away and he could barely move his tongue.

Kaz shrugged, but I saw in his eyes a reflection of my own horror that anyone, even someone as evil as Bryce, was forced to remain alive in this condition. For weeks now, his every moment had been agony; I was surprised that he hadn't gone insane.

"I'm sorry," I said, my voice softening. "I don't understand. You'll help us . . . right? Just nod if you can."

He ducked his chin a fraction of an inch but his gaping mouth worked, spittle forming at the corners, and he tried again. "Kihhh eee. Kihhh eee."

"He's saying 'kill me,'" Kaz said. "Is that right?"

Bryce managed a nod.

He wanted us to kill him. To put him out of his misery. I rested my trembling hands gently on the starched white linens of the bed. There was no way I could do what he asked, even if it was the humane choice.

But I could offer him something else.

"I can heal you," I whispered. "I don't know if I can . . . bring you all the way back. I've never— Your injuries are too . . . but I might be able to heal you enough."

It would be the greatest challenge I had faced as a Healer. I would not have attempted it a month earlier, or even a few days earlier. But I had healed Jess. I had healed Kaz. And each time I laid my hands on a wound, each time I felt the force within me summon itself and gather and strengthen as the voices murmured and swelled, I grew stronger.

And it wasn't just my skill that was growing. There was something else—something tied to my deepest understanding of who I was. The emotions that had defined me before I'd discovered my gift—fear, insecurity, hopelessness—were slipping away. In their place was a growing conviction that I could do the things that had been ordained for me, that I was a true and rightful Healer, and that my gift was meant to be used, and used well.

"We know you've been helping Prentiss reconstruct your work, but we need you to help us destroy it," Kaz said. "All the backups, everything."

"But it will take too long if we have to talk this way," I added. "I need to heal you."

"Nnnnn nnn nnn," Bryce gasped as tears formed at the

corners of his eyes, welling up and then coursing down his ruined face. He didn't want me to try to heal him, was terrified that I might bring him only partway back, forcing him to live like this indefinitely.

But there was no other way.

"I'm sorry," I said. "I have to touch you."

I closed my eyes and let the voices come, let the ancient rhythms spin and unfurl. The voices built until they reached my lips, and my need to say the words overwhelmed me. I tried to ignore Bryce's frantic, terrified mewling as I laid my shaking hand against his chest.

I was as gentle as I knew how to be, but my touch made him scream, the most horrible sound I had ever heard, pure pain compressed into a wail. I felt my own tears come as the words whispered forth from my lips and my blood danced and rushed with a stronger force than I'd ever felt.

This was different from any healing I'd done before. I could sense my gift's being drawn from further and further within the depths of my soul, stretched and taxed almost unbearably as I struggled to meet the challenge of Bryce's terrible wounds.

It was too much.

Under my hands, Bryce's flesh thrummed once, weakly, but then I felt the healing change course and excruciating pain shot backward into me, into the nerves of my fingers and along my arms into my very core, an agony so exquisite it was unlike anything I had known, anything I had imagined.

I wavered on the brink of consciousness. All I had to do was let go, take my hands off Bryce, and the pain would abate; it would slip back into the shadows like a rubber band released, like a wave racing back to the ocean. As I hesitated, the pain intensified, a burning raw rasp along every nerve ending in my body. Black spots danced in front of my eyes, and I heard nothing except for my own screams, but even they were locked inside. Since the pain was greater than my will, the pain ruled me, preventing me from making a sound.

I felt my fingers tremble against Bryce's body and I knew that the pain was going to win, that it was going to beat me. *I can't,* I said, or dreamed I said; I couldn't be sure. The voices were fading, the lyrical syllables chasing themselves into the darkness, a whisper, and then a sigh, almost gone, almost forgotten.

"Hailey." I heard Kaz's worried voice, but it was far away, so far away.

All I had to do was let go. There was no reason to be afraid. I would let go. I would send the pain hurtling back to the source, to Bryce. It would leave my body and seek its host, the burned and melted flesh of the man who had once sought to imprison me and use me to make zombies.

Bryce deserved the pain. He had brought it on himself.

He deserves this. . . .

I almost gave in. I nearly convinced myself to turn away. The voices had faded to a faint hum, and it was all I could do to keep from passing out. The black spots in my mind bloomed and ran together like a nightmare played at high speed.

But then something shifted.

I hadn't come this far, fought so hard, lost so much only to give up when I was tested. I might have questioned and even despised my gift; I might have wished it away. But it was as much a part of me as the heart that beat in my chest. It wasn't merely chance that had brought me together with the damaged and the wounded: I was *meant* to heal them. I was meant to use my gift.

"*Tá mé mol seo draíocht,*" I whispered, my lips trembling with the ancient words, and before I could draw another breath, the voices joined in, stronger than before, a chorus that wound up and down a beautiful dark scale, a harmony that only I could hear.

I gave in to the voices, but not before I tightened my fingers on Bryce's ruined flesh. I felt his body spasm with agony, but I held on.

"*Na anam an corp cara ár comhoibrí . . .*"

I saw nothing. The room fell away, and we were alone, me and Bryce and the ancients, my ancestors whose voices encouraged and strengthened me. Misgiving left me first, and then doubt, and finally pain; I felt nothing at all except for the energy flowing between my fingertips and Bryce. Other voices twined with the chant, speaking words I did not know: a man's voice, sure and gentle, and a woman's soft murmur in answer. I understood that they were the most ancient, the ones who had been there at the beginning. The original Banished were beside me, within me, guiding me, and in that moment I knew that they would be with me for the rest of my life.

And then I felt Bryce respond.

Just a tiny little tic, a blip in the flow of energy, but I'd felt it. I started the chant one last time, from the beginning, and as I spoke the words clear and strong, the other voices faded away, one by one, until the only one left was mine. I felt sorrow for their absence as my body returned to me. My vision flickered and I was aware of Kaz next to me, and there was a part of me that longed to follow the voices into the past, into a place that time and death could not reach, where I would be with my ancestors forever.

Then I heard Kaz whisper my name and I returned. I finished the verse and lifted my hands from Bryce, letting my exhausted body fall into Kaz's arms. As my vision cleared, I saw Bryce tremble and then go still. His flesh crackled with energy, his body sealing over the fissures on its own, repairing the cracked and blackened tissues, bursting forth with new cells.

I had done it. I had healed the man who'd tried to kill me and Prairie, the man who'd come closer to pure evil than anyone else I had met. Our struggles were far from over, and we were still in great danger.

But I had used my gift and used it well.

CHAPTER 36

I FELT STRONG ARMS AROUND ME and I knew that Kaz would not let me falter. He held me as I watched Bryce's tremors slowly subsiding. I couldn't judge how far Bryce had come, but he was better. His eyes no longer quivered in their sockets; he licked his restored lips; his exposed neck showed pink areas where healing appeared in the sheen of the flesh.

"Are you all right?" Kaz demanded.

I nodded. I felt fine—better, in fact, than I had before I touched Bryce. "We need to go."

"Yeah. Look, Safian, we're out of here. It's gonna hurt like hell and we can't be dragging all this crap along, so you're just going to have to hope that what Hailey did was enough."

I pushed Kaz gently away. I could stand on my own, and I was ready to run on my own, and fast. I had no idea how much longer we had before someone figured out what we were up to and came after us.

"We need a laptop."

"You heard her," Kaz said to Dr. Grace, who had been watching with a combination of fascination and horror. He handed me the gun and started shoving the equipment away from Bryce's bed, yanking out the tubes and peeling back the gauze from his body to free the IVs in his arms.

I kept the gun pointed at Dr. Grace while I scanned the room, spotting a laptop sitting on a desk crowded with papers. The program open on the screen made no sense to me, a chart with dozens of data points and a lot of scientific language along the bottom—but that didn't matter.

"I'm guessing this is password protected, right?" I asked Dr. Grace. "But I bet you have an override."

She shook her head. "No, sorry, I—"

Something in me snapped. My new strength was accompanied by an impatience that bordered on rage. We hadn't been through this much only to stop now. I pointed the gun directly at Dr. Grace's heart and said, "Try again. I'm not as patient as he is."

Reluctantly she went to the computer and typed a quick series of keystrokes. "I disabled password protection," she said.

"Launch the browser."

She did so, and when I was satisfied that it worked, I snapped the laptop shut and tucked it under my arm.

"So you don't need me now," Dr. Grace said. "I've given

you the password, and you have Bryce. Go, and I'll stay here, and I promise I won't sound the alarm. You can even lock me in here, and by the time they find me, you'll be long gone."

"Nice try," Kaz snapped. "But you're coming with us. Just in case we run into any trouble with the computer."

"I don't know anything more about the programs than I just showed you," she protested.

"Don't sell yourself short," I said sarcastically, but I didn't mention the other plan I had for her. Once we had destroyed the data, I was going to make Dr. Grace help us free Chub.

"Let's go," Kaz said, rolling Bryce's hospital bed away from the wall. Bryce had quieted down, and I could see perspiration on his face, on the skin that looked almost human again.

"Take us to your car," Kaz ordered Dr. Grace.

"I don't have a—"

I pulled her keys out and shook them in her face. I had noticed the logo on one of them. "It's an Audi, Dr. Grace. Does that refresh your memory? And do you really want to take your chances with me now that you know how easily I can put you out?"

She shook her head, fear showing in her eyes.

"So why don't you tell me about your car?"

"It's a . . . uh, an A4. White."

"That's better," I said, pocketing the keys again.

"I know I don't need to tell you this," Kaz said, "but take us by whatever route passes the fewest people."

Dr. Grace nodded, and after I checked to make sure the

hall was empty, she led us through a part of the building I hadn't yet seen. We took an elevator down two floors to a subbasement, the cinder-block walls and concrete floors lit by fluorescent lights, and after another brief walk, we took a freight elevator back up and paused in front of a set of double doors.

"This leads to the garage," Dr. Grace said. "Go ahead."

I turned Dr. Grace's key in the lock and was getting ready to push when Kaz stopped me.

"No. Wait. How do we know it's really the garage? She could have brought us anywhere."

I stared at the doors, the freshly painted surfaces, the gleaming hardware and realized that Kaz had a point.

I rolled Bryce's bed backward, away from the door, but while Kaz hesitated, Dr. Grace threw herself at the doors and they crashed open, revealing a windowless room where three men worked at desks. In a fraction of a second, they bolted from their chairs and reached for their weapons. One hit the floor and rolled, and another fired at the doorframe, sending splinters flying.

"Get them!" Dr. Grace yelled, but we were already on the move. Kaz shoved her from behind, propelling her into the room, and I threw the doors shut. I heard a scream on the other side and realized that Dr. Grace had been hit.

Kaz yanked the bed linens off Bryce, revealing his wasted body in a hospital gown, and muttered "Sorry" before lifting Bryce over his shoulder. I flinched when Bryce cried out from the pain.

"Come on!" Kaz yelled, and we dashed back down the hall, the laptop heavy under my arm. We rounded a corner and saw that the freight elevator was still waiting with open doors, and we threw ourselves into it and I jabbed at the Close button. In seconds we were descending again.

I was half expecting the doors to open on someone pointing a gun in our faces, but the corridor was still eerily quiet. Bryce moaned as Kaz shifted his weight on his shoulders.

"This way," I said, guessing. A door marked AUTHORIZED PERSONNEL ONLY was propped open. I felt for a switch, found a bank of lights and shoved them all on.

Kaz followed me into the room and I kicked the doorstop out of the way. The door slammed and we were alone—and safe, for the moment.

We were in the industrial heart of the building, a cavernous room housing massive heating and cooling units with dozens of huge white pipes curving into the ceiling. Ladders and fire extinguishers were mounted on the wall. The equipment hummed, echoing off the concrete floors.

"I'm setting you down," Kaz said, easing Bryce to the floor and then standing painfully, massaging the strain from his shoulders. Bryce flopped like a rag doll and lay still.

"We can't take him out of the building now," I said. I knew they must be sounding the alarm throughout the building, trying to find us. "You have to do it here."

"But he's out," Kaz said.

I knelt down next to him. "I'll just heal him a little more," I said. "Then I have to go."

"Go *where?*"

"To get Rattler and Prairie. I've been thinking about what you said."

"You can't go out there now," Kaz protested. "It's too dangerous."

"I have to. We need them to help us get Chub out."

"But there's—"

"And you have to stay here with Bryce and make him help you destroy it all."

Our eyes locked for a moment, Kaz's fear for me battling his determination, and then he nodded. There was no other way.

CHAPTER 37

THERE WAS A DIAGRAM on the wall that showed the heating and cooling infrastructure throughout the building. "See if you can figure out a route to the garage," I suggested.

And then I took Bryce's hand.

I was pretending bravado I didn't feel, but as I bent over Bryce, I forgot my fears and focused on making him just a little bit better. I had to be careful; I would be no good to anyone if I let the healing sap too much of my strength. I needed only to keep Bryce conscious and alert.

For the first time ever, I was aware of holding back. I had said the words often enough that they came automatically to my lips, and I envisioned a barrier in my mind, a black velvet curtain lowering and sealing off most of my energy, releasing only enough of my gift to settle and calm Bryce's overtaxed heart, to restore enough health to his lungs and throat that he could breathe and talk.

And then I pulled back. I sensed the gift returning to me, and swallowed the healing words.

But it had helped. Bryce's skin looked better, and a downy fuzz of hair had appeared on his skull. His eyes were bright and alert, and he licked his lips and raised his hand to scratch at his neck. He no longer seemed to be drowning in pain.

"Mr. Safian," I said carefully, worried that he would turn back into a ruthless maniac now that he was feeling better, "you must help Kaz now. You need to tell him the commands to wipe out your remote backups. Can you do that?"

For a moment he said nothing and I wondered what we would do if he refused. Now that I had brought him some relief from his suffering, I doubted he would be as cooperative. Not only might he have decided he no longer wanted to die—but he might be eager to protect his life's work.

"I will do that," he said, his voice sounding rusty from lack of use.

"It's really important," I said. "You have to make sure that—"

"No more," Bryce rasped. "No more healing, no more zombies." He pointed to himself. "I was wrong. I deserved to die. The things I have seen them do, since they brought me here—evil things. I never understood . . . I'm sorry. I'm so sorry."

His hand lifted weakly off the floor and he pressed his

fingers to my face. They were barely warm, but I didn't pull away.

"How can I believe you?" I asked.

"Before, I wanted . . . money . . . power. Since I came here, I have wanted only to die. I never sleep, the pain keeps me awake, and I think of those young men . . . every one of them. They never leave me."

I didn't know what to say. His regret seemed genuine, the tears sparkling in his eyes real. I wanted to believe. But after everything he had done . . .

"Hailey, you have to go *now*," Kaz said. "We'll be fine here. Come take a look at this."

He led me to the diagram and showed me that the garage was located directly above us, one floor below ground level.

"Look here," Kaz said, pointing to a box with an X in the far corner of the square labeled "HVAC." "This vent goes straight into the garage."

He pointed to the corner of the room, where a large square grate had been installed in the ceiling.

"You want me to crawl up there?" I asked skeptically. "That's got to be fifteen feet off the ground."

Kaz pointed to the ladders.

At first the task seemed hopeless, even with the ladder we dragged over. My fingertips barely touched the grate. I could reach one of the clips holding the grate in place, but even if we moved the ladder so I could loosen each of them, I'd still have no way to get up there.

"I need your help," I said. "A boost . . ."

237

I climbed down to the floor, and Kaz hoisted me onto his shoulders. I blushed when he grabbed my ankles to keep me steady, but he didn't seem to mind. He climbed the ladder slowly, my hands wrapped tightly under his chin, until he was standing on the top step.

Now that I could reach all the clips, I worked at them frantically. Looking down was scary, and several times Kaz wavered and I almost lost my balance.

But Healers aren't like ordinary people. We're stronger, faster, hardier, and more coordinated, and when the last of the clips clattered to the floor, I reached up for one of the braces holding the ceiling in place. I gripped it tightly and swung myself up, sliding my feet into the opening and scooting into the tight space. I blinked away cobwebs and saw that beyond the opening was a large hollow vent.

"Go," I said to Kaz. "You have to hurry."

"Wait, Hailey."

I turned, my hair falling in my face, and saw him framed in the opening, his gray eyes flickering with uncertainty.

"Just . . . be careful," he finally said, and held up his hand. I reached back down, and our fingers touched for a second. I closed my eyes and let the energy travel between us, the attraction of the Banished, the strength of our blood and our history.

And then I pushed forward as though all our lives depended on it.

CHAPTER 38

SOON, SOON.

Hailey had come to see him and that was good and Kaz came and that was good too. He showed Hailey the book with the worm. He wanted to show Hailey the book with the spider but Hailey and Kaz had to go, Hailey had to fix the Monster Man and Kaz had to help.

Chub was ready, but he was scared. He had a mind-picture of where he had to go, and he had to go soon, and he hadn't had a chance to tell Hailey. He had to go, the mind-picture showed him where. That way and then turn and turn and turn. Big room, box piles, all the boxes and the cans. The door at the end. The door at the end was open and that was where he had to go.

Chub was scared, but he knew he wouldn't get in trouble. He was scared and he wished he could have told Hailey where he had to go. But the mind-picture didn't come until after she left. He wasn't going to tell anyone else. Something was wrong with the lady with the brown glasses. She wasn't coming. Someone else would come.

Soon, soon. Chub stood right next to the door, hide hide hide because when the person came he was going to run fast. The mind-picture showed him where to go and he would be fast, and the person would not be fast enough to catch him.

Chub waited, ready to run.

CHAPTER 39

THE SUN WAS SINKING into the horizon when I pulled out onto the road, the car bucking and lurching in my uncertain hands. The brakes on Dr. Grace's car were far more sensitive than the ones on Prairie's Camry, and the steering wheel spun too easily, making the car swerve and dip as I barreled down the road away from the office park.

The garage had been nearly empty when I popped the grate only a dozen yards from where I'd climbed into the ceiling. I'd counted fewer than two dozen cars, and it had been easy to find the Audi. I didn't see anyone as I drove it out of the complex, but I knew the garage was monitored, and I didn't know how much of a lead I could count on.

I half expected to see headlights in my rearview mirror, but I had an advantage: sixteen years in Gypsum, sixteen years of exploring every road and field and farm. So I knew exactly which roads intersected others, which dirt tracks over-grown with weeds led to leaning barns and which to short-cuts to neighboring land.

I took a looping, haphazard route, and when I finally wound back to State Road 9, there was no one behind me, no telltale dust cloud—nothing at all except the purple evening sky, the first fireflies of the night dancing in the air.

When I passed the house I had lived in until a few months earlier, I saw that all the windows had been broken. Plywood was nailed over a few of them, but the front door had been ripped from the hinges and a sodden pile of torn-out carpet lay in the yard.

Everyone in town knew that Gram had dealt drugs, and not long ago three people had died here. No wonder some-one had trashed the place. Before I could think of a single thing to miss about the old house, it was in my rearview mir-ror, and the thickening evening obscured the woods as I drove the last mile to the edge of Trashtown. I eased the car to the side of the road and watched the lights winking on in the rows of shacks lining both sides of Morrin Street.

The Morries all lived here, the scrawny mean-eyed boys with dirt under their nails, the pale mumbling girls with long stringy hair obscuring their faces. There were fifteen, maybe twenty, Morrie kids in my old high school; more in the younger grades, sullen brothers and sisters whose past was en-twined with mine and Prairie's, even Anna's and Kaz's. Their futures were bleak; their weak Banished blood condemned them to meanness and shiftlessness and addiction, hardscrabble lives lived out here in Trashtown. Few would escape, the way Prairie had. Or even the way I had, by accident.

The Morries had always hated me, though maybe not as much as they hated Gram, even while their fathers and uncles and older brothers fell further and further into her debt, buying her weed and prescription drugs. Maybe they blamed me for that.

If the Morries knew about Prentiss's plan to round up the Seers and put them to work, they might even be pleased. Prentiss would pay them—far more than they got from the state or from their occasional construction and factory jobs. With the lab right here in town, it would be almost like an office job, the kind for which they were routinely passed over.

For a moment despair clouded my mind, pressing against my temples, making my breath come in ragged gasps. Not ten miles away, Chub was still trapped, and Kaz was in danger. But I was the only one who could help now. And I would do what needed to be done.

I put the car in gear again and lurched down Morrin Street. I thought of the very few times I'd been brave enough to ride my bike around the edges of Trashtown, before I knew I was Banished, spying on the people who lived there as they went about their lives, longing to join them and not understanding why. Now that I was finally on the inside, it looked even more broken down, more desperate. Junker cars and trucks were parked in the dirt; porches sagged; roofs were missing shingles.

Even in the twilight, I knew Rattler's truck the minute I

passed it. He'd driven the old green Ford around town for years. It seemed as though it was held together by rust. The sound of its grinding gears and worn-out muffler used to be enough to set my heart pounding with fear.

But now I was relieved to see it. I parked behind it and trailed my hand along the side as I hurried past it to the house. The hood was warm; the truck had been driven recently.

The lawn hadn't been mowed in weeks, and my shoes slapped against the weedy grass. I took the rotting, uneven porch steps with care. The house was no different from its neighbors, weathered wood showing through the peeling paint, an old black iron mailbox hanging at an angle from a single nail, an overturned bucket the only object on the sloped porch. Through a limp gray curtain, a weak light shined, but the upper windows were dark. I smelled mildew and garbage and smoke.

I took a breath and thought of Chub and Prairie and raised my hand to knock. Before my fist could strike the door, it opened and I was staring into the harsh-planed face and spinning milky eye of Rattler Sikes. It was like he had been waiting there for me, still as a snake, ready to strike.

"Hailey-girl," he said softly. "Come to see your papa."

Prairie stepped from the shadows. She pushed Rattler out of the way and gathered me into her arms with a soft cry, and I knew her from her scent, from her silky hair, from the tight embrace that seemed as though it would go on forever.

When she finally released me, her voice was choked with tears of relief. "Thank God," she breathed.

And I almost broke.

"Prairie, I—" There were a thousand things I wanted to say to her, most of them apologies. I was sorry I'd lied to her. Sorry I'd thought I could protect us better than she could. Sorry I'd taken her for granted, sorry I'd let evil find us, sorry I hadn't been there for her. But there wasn't time, so I settled for the most important. "I love you."

Rattler raised his hand, and I flinched, waiting for the blow—but he only turned on a light switch, illuminating a neat parlor with furniture that looked like it was a century old, the arms covered with crocheted doilies, and wood floors swept clean.

"My girls," he said, as though it amused him.

"We've struck a deal," Prairie said stiffly.

"What do you mean?" I asked.

"Rattler had a vision, Hailey. All of you, out at Quadrillon. He says trouble's coming tonight."

"Big trouble," Rattler echoed. "Death dealin' and blood runnin'."

"You're going to help us?" I demanded.

"Hell yes I am," Rattler drawled. "Fact, we were just on our way when you showed up. I got the truck loaded up ready."

Prairie steered me back onto the porch. "We need to go. We can talk on the way."

Only then did I see that she had a belt slung around her waist that was clearly too big, a holster holding a handgun clipped to the front. I gasped, and Prairie's expression turned grim.

"Why—how—"

"It's Rattler's," she said. "He's got one for you, too, Hailey."

"What exactly is this deal you made?"

She looked deep into my eyes, her expression sad. "You don't need to know the particulars, Hailey."

"Oh, yes I do," I protested, refusing to step out of her way.

Prairie sighed and put her hand to her throat, and I knew she was touching the ruby pendant that matched mine.

"All right," she finally said. "Rattler's going to help us get Chub out. We'll find Kaz. And the three of you will go back to Chicago. Rattler's promised he won't look for you there ever again. You'll be free, Hailey."

"But what about you?" I asked, my blood suddenly running cold.

Because I already knew the answer. I knew the deal that Prairie had made.

She'd traded herself to Rattler to buy our freedom.

CHAPTER 40

RATTLER DROVE STRAIGHT through town, not bothering to disguise his route. I knew that people got out of the way when they saw Rattler's truck coming, because any encounter with Rattler was bad news, whether you were Banished or not. No one followed us; it was past the dinner hour now and people were at home for the night.

The truck's shocks had seen better days and every jolt and bump jarred my spine, but Rattler didn't seem to mind. I was wedged against the passenger door. Between us, Prairie rode with her hands folded in her lap and her head held high. I knew better than to try to argue with her now, but I couldn't believe she had agreed to stay with Rattler once this night was done.

She'd done it for me and Chub. And for Anna and Kaz. She'd done it so that Rattler would never come after us, never drag us back to Trashtown to live out our lives in poverty and abuse. I felt sick at heart knowing what she was willing to sacrifice to save us.

I told her almost everything. About how sorry I was that we'd left her behind. About our pulling over to rest and Rattler and Derek's finding us. About surviving the explosion only to end up in Prentiss's new headquarters. About seeing Chub, and Dr. Grace, and Bryce and about the terrible thing Prentiss had asked me to do. About nearly falling for the trap and escaping to the utility room, and about Kaz's plan to destroy the data before we got back.

There were a few things I didn't tell her about. Like the night Kaz and I had stayed in the motel, and the kiss we'd shared. And the room Rattler had set up for her, with the photo of the two of them when they were children. Those things I saved to tell her later, because that way I could pretend that there would be a later, that she would be leaving with me when everything was over.

Throughout the trip, Rattler drove with a half smile on his face. Every now and then he rested one of his big callused hands on Prairie's knee. It was as though he was trying to reassure himself that she was really there, as though he didn't quite trust his spinning eye not to conjure her image from nothing.

If Rattler was afraid, he didn't show it. And if Prairie was afraid, her fear had little to do with the next few hours—and much to do with what would follow.

We fell silent as we pulled off the road. We approached

the circular drive in front of the complex on foot, staying in the shadows cast by the decorative landscape lighting. The foyer was dark, the reception desk empty, but I knew that inside, a frantic search was going on, if it hadn't already concluded with Kaz's capture.

I was waiting for the doors to open with shouts and gunfire when a small figure shot out of the bushes and came running toward us at a gallop, then collided with me, nearly knocking me down.

"Hayee!"

It was Chub. We tumbled together, hugging each other, Chub babbling excitedly, me holding on for dear life. Prairie was next; she scooped him up and kissed his cheeks, his forehead. He laughed and shrieked with delight—and then, suddenly, he stopped.

He regarded Rattler solemnly from the safety of Prairie's arms. "Your eye hurts."

Rattler chuckled. "No, little man, it don't. This here's a magic eye. It tells me tales."

But Chub shook his head and ducked his chin. "It hurts," he repeated. "It makes you sad."

Rattler's grin faltered, but he played along, winking at Chub. "I ain't sad. You're lookin' at a man what's about to do what he does best. Gonna bust some ass and take what's mine is what we're fixin' to do."

"We can't take Chub in there with us," I protested.

"He can wait in the truck," Rattler said. "Jes' as soon's he shows us how he got out here in the first place."

We followed Chub back along a brick path that wound behind lattice screens, thick with wisteria. Shielded from view, the path took a turn toward the back of the complex, where Dumpsters were clustered next to a loading dock. The air smelled of garbage, and flies buzzed.

"I saw that, I saw that door," Chub said proudly, pointing. Sure enough, a door stood open. Trash bags were stacked haphazardly outside, as though someone had been interrupted in the middle of a task.

By an alarm sounding through the complex, for instance.

"I'll take the young'un back," Rattler said, reaching for Chub. But Chub backed away from him, clearly frightened. "Oh, now, I won't hurt you none," Rattler crooned.

The sound curdled my blood. My father's voice was not one that would ever sing a lullaby or soothe an injured child. There was no comfort in it, and Chub—who knew far more than most little boys—didn't trust it.

Not until I told him to. I hated doing it, but there was no other way.

"Chub, you go with Mr. Sikes now," I said, kneeling down to give him a hug and a kiss. "You get to sit in his nice big truck and wait just a little while and then I'll be back for you. Lie down and try to sleep, and maybe you'll have a nice dream."

Chub looked skeptical, but he reluctantly went to Rattler.

Rattler was back in moments. We were barely inside the building when we heard a woman's scream.

CHAPTER 41

I HAD BECOME FAMILIAR enough with the layout of the place to know that the scream came from the direction of the atrium at the center of the complex.

I led the way, fear boosting my adrenaline. Behind me, Rattler jogged along, holding weapons in both hands. I didn't know guns, so I wasn't sure what they were, but one looked like a regular handgun, and the other like something out of a video game, big and heavy.

The scream came again, stark with horror and fear. Dr. Grace's voice, it sounded like. As we rounded the last turn, I saw that I was right: Dr. Grace, her hands bound behind her, was standing on a circular coffee table, turning one way and then another, nearly tripping herself in her panic. A red stain on one shoulder revealed where she'd been shot. It looked like the bullet hadn't done much damage. It certainly wasn't the reason she was screaming.

Circling the table where she stood was a ring of zombies.

"Holy . . . ," I heard Rattler mutter behind me, and just in time I turned to see him raising both his weapons in the air.

"Don't," I said. "You can't kill them like that!"

Rattler glared at me, but he didn't shoot, and we stopped at the edge of the atrium, stunned by the scene.

Dr. Grace was not alone. Bryce had been propped up on the floor against the coffee table, at Dr. Grace's feet. He was conscious, his eyes tracking the action in the room, and his color was returning as his flesh continued to knit. Next to him crouched Kaz, pleading with Dr. Grace in a low voice, telling her to stay calm.

Many of the chairs in the room were occupied, and I recognized the staff I'd encountered over the last couple of days. Biceps. Texas. The servers from the cafeteria, the security staff, the researchers I'd passed in the halls. And up front, standing on a huge flagstone hearth, was Prentiss, watching the proceedings as though they amused him. He caught my eye and gave me a chilling smile.

"Hailey!" Prentiss called. "How delightful to see you. And Prairie, what a nice surprise. I had hoped to welcome you personally, but things did get fouled up, didn't they? Nevertheless, we are pleased you could make it. And Mr. Sikes. My intrepid partner." His voice turned cold. "You've supplied me with one . . . challenge after another."

"Shut your mouth, you damn windbag," Rattler snapped. "You got what's mine. One a my people. Let 'im go now, and we'll be on our way."

"Your people . . ." Prentiss pretended to be confused. "Oh, you must mean young Mr. Sawicki. I am afraid I will be requiring his services. In fact, we were just having a . . . staff meeting, to introduce him. And, of course, to discipline Dr. Grace, who was careless enough to allow him and young Hailey to cause quite a disruption. And now you've brought the Tarbells to join us. How very expedient."

Kaz had gotten to his feet and clambered up onto the coffee table, where he was trying to quiet Dr. Grace. He shot me a smile that didn't reach his eyes.

"I'm'a start shootin' now," Rattler said. "I'll drop one a your folks at a time until you start talkin' sense."

Before anyone could react, a shot echoed through the space and there was a sharp exclamation; the man who had served me my lunch the day before fell to the carpet, clutching his arm and moaning. I hadn't even seen him move.

"Jes' so you know, if I'd'a meant to kill 'im, he'd be a dead man," Rattler added placidly.

Prentiss chuckled. "Impressive, I suppose, when one hails from a backwater town such as this. Only don't forget, my dear man, that I'm always a step ahead of you."

He motioned with his outstretched arms, and the staff rose from their seats.

"Endearing, really, your bravado," Prentiss said. On the floor the injured man moaned and clutched his elbow.

"Especially when my men could exterminate you in three seconds flat. Oh yes, on my signal they—"

Rattler's guns exploded a second time, several bursts in quick succession. A man fell from the second-floor balcony, hitting the ground with a sickening thud, and another lurched from the shadows across the room, took two tottering steps, and fell in a spray of his own blood.

For a moment Rattler and Prentiss stared at each other, and then Prentiss continued in a tight voice, as though Rattler hadn't just shot two of his guards. "Are ready to act on my command, is what I was going to say, Mr. Sikes. My men are disciplined. They respond only to my orders. Although if you really want to see impressive loyalty, you need only look to the subjects of my study. My passion, you might call them, the results of millions of dollars and years of research, the fruit of a collaborative effort that your own people, as you call them, have made possible."

There was silence as all eyes turned to the zombies, who had stayed motionless.

Prentiss walked slowly across the room. "Gentlemen," he said when he was only a few feet from the ring of zombies. "Seize the Tarbells."

The gasp that went up throughout the room echoed my own shock. I staggered backward to Prairie and grabbed her hand, and we held tightly to each other. I frantically searched the room for an escape, but the only exits were blocked by Prentiss's men.

The zombies did not hurry. They shambled, their steps

uncertain and almost comic, the motions of a drunkard. Their hands reached out toward us and their mouths opened with flesh lust, and I heard my own whimper of fear.

"No."

Another voice rasped out, and the zombies slowed. They turned, one after another, tottering on their rotting limbs, staring without emotion at the source of the voice.

Bryce.

He had managed to drag himself into one of the chairs, his face red with exertion. "No. Do not do what Prentiss says. No, wait—go to Prentiss. Now."

"Stop," Prentiss barked.

"You forgot," Bryce said. "All the training protocols, the recordings, the sessions . . . whose voice were they in, General?"

"Don't call me that," Prentiss protested, his cultivated voice going high and thin.

"Oh, but that's what I *always* called you, back in the day," Bryce said. With effort, he pushed himself into a standing position, leaning against the chair for support. "'The General.' You used to like it, don't you remember? Made you feel important. Made you feel like you were a part of the team."

The zombies approached Prentiss, clustering together like a second-grade class on a field trip.

"But you were *never* part of the team, General," Bryce went on. It seemed almost like he was starting to enjoy the conversation. "*I* was the one who made it work. *I* was the one who figured out the impossible. And now *I'm* the one who has destroyed it all. You hear me, General? It's gone, every last backup. The boy and I made sure of it. And now it's time for you to be gone too."

Prentiss's mouth worked in terror, but nothing came out.

"No one will grieve you when you're gone," Bryce continued. "No one will remember you at all. Didn't you ever learn, General, that pride's a sin?"

One of the men at the periphery had been stealthily advancing, creeping along the bases of the chairs, trying to get a clear shot at Rattler. As Bryce rambled on, Rattler suddenly whipped around toward the creeping guard and took his shot, and the guard fell to the carpet.

"Pride's a sin," Bryce repeated, almost reflectively. "And I guess no one knows that more than me. Deactivate Alistair Prentiss, please."

Prentiss stood his ground for ten, maybe even twenty, seconds, sputtering and making threats, before he turned and tried to bolt from the room. But he'd gone only a step or two before Rattler shot the ground at his feet, and he spun and cried out in fear.

After that, it was just a matter of waiting.

We all waited: the staff, cowering in their small groups, clutching each other for comfort; me and Prairie, who had never let go; Kaz, who wrapped his arms around Dr. Grace to block out the sounds.

Most of all, Prentiss waited, his eyes going twitchy with terror as the first of the zombies set upon him.

I won't describe the rest. I turned away after a few seconds. The zombies kept coming, relentless, and it was a mercy that they set upon his throat first, so we didn't have to listen to his screams.

It was over fast. When Prentiss was dead, the pack dropped him to the floor without ceremony, their task finished, and then Bryce's voice was heard again.

"Now come to me."

They started across the floor, festooned with Prentiss's blood, and Bryce stood tall and proud, a slight tremor the only evidence of his body's frail state. The zombies circled him in an ever-tightening scrum, and when they were so close that they bumped into each other, he took a deep breath and spoke in a calm voice.

"Open those doors and take me down into the waters with you and keep me there until the breath has left us all."

I opened my mouth to protest. Prairie tensed and held me even more tightly. But no one tried to stop them.

The zombies did as they were told. They were not humans anymore, just flesh sacks that could follow orders, and they picked up Bryce as though he weighed nothing and carried him out the glass doors overlooking the pond. It was lovely in the moonlight, its blue-black surface broken only by the occasional water bug. Our view through the spotless windows was perfectly clear as the zombies held Bryce aloft like a treasured trophy and walked into the water.

Indifferent, they waded through the cluster of lily pads. Then they began to submerge, one by one, their expressionless faces sinking into the moonlit water up to their chins, their noses and finally their eyes, until those too were extinguished.

At last it was only Bryce who remained, cradled in a dozen decaying hands, and then even his serene face slipped below. Bubbles rose to the surface and then disappeared.

I trembled with the horror of what I'd witnessed. But now I knew: Bryce really had repented in the end. He'd done the one thing that would prevent anyone from forcing him to replicate his work ever again. He'd given Kaz the passwords, and together they'd wiped out the data once and for all.

"Anyone else?" Rattler demanded. I'd noticed the staff slipping away one by one toward the doors, skirting the mess that had been Prentiss. Kaz gave Dr. Grace a little push, and she stumbled after the others.

"I said, anyone else want to step up?" Rattler demanded again. "No? We'll be leaving, then. I imagine your little deal with the townfolk's officially over now. This place'll be crawlin' soon, and I was you, I guess I'd be trying to get outta here."

Kaz reached for my hand and drew me close. I hugged him hard, making room for Prairie to join us, but she didn't—and then I saw that Rattler was holding her hand tightly.

When her gaze met my eyes, for a moment I thought I saw something of her old spirit there—a flash of defiance—before she turned away. But then her shoulders slumped as she trailed behind Rattler.

She was his now. She had bought our freedom with her promise.

CHAPTER 42

CHUB HAD FALLEN ASLEEP in the cab of Rattler's truck, curled up with his fist pressed to his cheek. He woke when I opened the door. Then he yawned and held up his arms. Prairie picked him up and held him close, and he wrapped his arms around her neck and went back to sleep as she kissed him.

"I'll ride up front," Prairie said.

She had directed her words to Rattler, who was stowing his firearms in a metal box behind the seat, but there was a note of uncertainty in her voice.

She was asking his permission.

My heart constricted. This was her new life, then; Rattler was now her mate and her master, and she would have to beg for every favor and freedom.

She'd done it for me. And Kaz and Anna and Chub.

I wanted to protest, to tell her that she and I would take our chances together. I had survived too much to be afraid, and I'd go anywhere with Prairie, face anything. And I knew Kaz would too. But the problem was that it wasn't just us.

Rattler snapped the lid of the box and spun the padlock, then put a hand on the driver door and considered Prairie, who was shivering in the cool of the evening.

"You ride next to me. Put the boy on your lap. You two, in back."

Prairie complied without a word, settling Chub onto her lap, where he snuggled in and fell back asleep. Kaz shut her door gently.

Then it was just me and Kaz. Out on the road I saw the first of the cars peeling out of the garage. County fire and emergency would not be here for a while, I guessed, since Prentiss had no doubt paid them handsomely to keep their distance. Eventually, though, they would come, and they would find the place deserted except for the bodies in the atrium. Bryce and the zombies would wash up on the edges of the pond. Depending how long it took, maybe their decomposition would be chalked up to the time in the water.

One thing was sure: no one would ever know what had really happened here.

Bryce and Prentiss were dead. The research was finally destroyed. The Banished, once again, would be free to live their lives in peace.

Kaz offered me a hand, and we scrambled up the bumper into the truck bed. The cold wind whipped our faces, but Kaz wrapped his arms around me and I closed my eyes and held on.

CHAPTER 43

BUT THE TRUCK DIDN'T MOVE.

I waited, shivering in Kaz's arms, for the engine to turn over. Off to the west of the office park I saw a bobbing, flickering light. Someone had had the sense to find a flashlight before running. Good for them—they'd be glad to have it when the moon went behind a cloud.

After several long moments, the passenger door opened and Prairie got out, carrying Chub. He was sleeping soundly, loose as a rag doll in her arms.

"Get out, hurry," she said. "I need you to hold him."

"What about—"

"Rattler's taken care of." Prairie cut me off, flashing me a quick, humorless smile. "Come on, Hailey, that trick you pulled with Maynard?"

"What—"

"You're not the only girl in town who can do that," Prairie added. "Only I did it with a kiss."

I imagined how it had gone: Rattler, alone with his love at last, Chub sleeping between them. Rattler, unable to wait, stealing a kiss before he took her home to start his new empire.

The determination and loathing I'd glimpsed, which she'd kept coiled and hidden all through her ordeal, bursting free, coursing through her body into his. Intensified by the blood bond between them, the eternal attraction of the Banished.

"Hurry," Prairie urged, and Kaz and I scrambled out of the truck bed. I took Chub from her and hitched him up on my shoulder as she leaned back into the truck and rooted around behind the seat.

When she straightened, she was holding one of Rattler's guns—the smaller one, which still seemed plenty big to me. It looked at home in her hand and I realized that I'd never asked her if she knew how to shoot.

She seemed to read my mind as she gestured at Rattler with the gun. He was slumped over the steering wheel, his arms limp at his sides. "Who do you think taught me?" she asked, her voice as hard and cold as steel. "Him and Dun Acey. First it was BB guns in the woods. Didn't take long to move on from there."

She took aim and I almost stopped her, because I was remembering the photo in the room Rattler had prepared for her: two skinny kids playing in the creek. The look of

263

longing on his face as she sparkled and danced in the sun. He'd been a dangerous and reckless child; he'd grown into a dangerous and twisted man. But he had loved her always and that love refused to die.

He was my father, but he'd never loved me. Only one woman would ever shine for him, and every terrible thing he'd done since I met him, he'd done for her.

That was my last thought before she shot him.

CHAPTER 44

PRAIRIE WANTED TO LEAVE HIM THERE, lying in the dirt outside the office park. She figured his death would be chalked up as one more casualty of the night's violence, and I knew she was right.

But I insisted we take him home to die.

He never regained consciousness. Blood bubbled from his nostrils and trailed from his slack mouth. Prairie had shot him in the chest, and there was a rattling wheeze as he struggled to breathe.

We laid him out in the passenger seat, and I held Chub on my lap in the back with Kaz as Prairie drove through town and into the darkened streets of Trashtown.

Curtains moved and lights flickered in the windows of the houses along Morrin Street. Despite the late hour, people were up: restless souls looking for a high; bitter men looking for a target for their anger; fearful women hiding in their own homes. The Audi was still parked in front of Rattler's house where I'd left it, and I imagined that everyone in town had noticed it and wondered who had come to call. Unsettled by indecipherable waking dreams of water and blood, the Seers would have known something was coming.

Prairie parked and we got out of the truck. Chub slept on, oblivious. Kaz opened the passenger door, and our eyes met.

"I'll carry him in. Why don't you and Prairie get in the Audi with Chub—I'll be right back."

"*No.*" The firmness of my voice surprised me. "I'm coming."

No one spoke for a moment. Prairie slowly got out of the car, wiping blood from her arm. She stared at Rattler like she'd never seen him before. And I realized that in a way, she hadn't; at least, she'd never looked at him without fear before, never known him when he wasn't a danger to her.

"Give Prairie the keys," Kaz said gently.

I did; then I handed Chub over, and Prairie cradled him in her arms and walked slowly toward the Audi without looking back.

It was down to Kaz and me. He dragged Rattler from the car and got him over his shoulders in a fireman's carry. It took effort; Rattler was solidly built, every ounce of him muscle and bone. I walked ahead, and when we reached the front door, I knew the knob would turn in my hand. I'd guessed that Rattler would not lock his home, that he would not be afraid of any threat that could come through his front door.

I was right.

Inside, I snapped on a light switch and the front parlor was lit with the ocher glow from a china lamp on a battered hutch. Even in the dim light I could see that Rattler had made an effort to prepare his home for Prairie. Every surface—the humble pine floors, the old furniture, the paneled walls—was scrubbed and gleaming. Yellowed lace-edged linens were draped over tables. Crumbling crocheted doilies covered chair backs. Jars of wildflowers lined the windowsills.

My heart hitched as Kaz laid Rattler on a faded sofa, his long legs extending far past the end. It had been important to me that my father die here, in his home, among the Banished. There was no love between us; I knew that. Besides Prairie and Chub, he was the only family I had left—but more important, he was my link to my ancestors, and the blood that ran in my veins was his blood. I owed at least some part of my strength, my determination, even my bravery to him.

As I knelt in front of him, I could feel the energy of the place, the low, thrumming, familiar heartbeat of my ancestors, who lived on in the very soil here. The blood shed in these streets was Banished blood; the tears that fell in the rooms of these shacks were Banished tears. Our people had gone terribly wrong since they'd left the ancient village centuries earlier, but as I watched my dying father take his last struggling breaths, I knew that I would never be able to turn my back on them, on who I was.

I looked up at Kaz. He was watching me, his expression full of concern.

"You're going to heal him," he whispered.

He knew it before I did, but once he said the words, my hands were already reaching for Rattler. I *was* going to heal him, not because I wanted to, but because I *had* to.

CHAPTER 45

COMPARED TO HEALING BRYCE, healing my father was simple. The words slipped from my lips; the energy traveled smoothly through my fingertips into his damaged flesh. Almost instantly I felt the jagged edge of the bullet wound begin to skim over.

Beginning the process was easy. Stopping it was hard. I took a deep breath, squeezed my eyes shut and wrenched my hands away in the middle of the verse. A splitting pain sliced through my head, and my hands twitched as though I'd been electrocuted. I almost fell, but Kaz crouched beside me and put his arms around me.

"What's wrong?" he demanded. "What happened?"

"I'm okay," I said hoarsely, disentangling myself from his arms and easing myself into a straight chair next to the sofa.

"I just need to talk to him for a minute. Would you mind . . . I need to do this alone."

Kaz hesitated, but he bent and kissed me on the forehead. "I'll be right outside," he whispered before stepping out onto the front porch.

Rattler was awake now, and he was watching me, his eyes narrowed and his mouth a tight line. I knew he was in a lot of pain; I could sense it in the connection between us. I also knew he would live if I left right now—if he got to a hospital quickly enough, if they took the bullet out, if he followed doctors' orders. I had not healed him all the way. I had stopped well shy of restoring his flesh. I'd slowed the leaking of his blood and I sensed that I had fixed something critical that had been severed—that much I could tell from the exchange of energy that ran between us.

"You'll be all right," I muttered. I didn't want Rattler to die; I didn't want his death on my conscience. I wasn't afraid of him, not really, not anymore. His gifts were strong, but so were mine. As hard as he fought for what he believed was rightfully his, I would fight harder if I needed to.

But there was Prairie to consider. And there was Chub.

I leaned closer so that our faces were only inches apart. Up close I saw how fine and unlined his skin still was. And something else: for the first time I noticed that his nose, his chin, his eyebrows—all of them were similar to mine.

He was, unquestionably, my father. But I owed him nothing.

"You can't have her," I said softly.

He started to speak, then grimaced with pain. When he tried again, it was through gritted teeth. "B-b- . . . bitch shot me."

"She'll do it again," I said. "And so will I. If you ever—*ever*—threaten any of us again. If you so much as show your face to me or her, or Chub or Kaz or Anna. This is your one chance. Next time I let you die."

Rattler's eyes sparked with fury and his mouth curled with contempt. "I'd li . . . li . . . like to see you try," he said, and then he passed out.

His words barely registered. In my mind, I was already long gone.

EPILOGUE

JULY 4

THEY WERE SETTING FIREWORKS OFF over the lake tonight. Kaz told me about it—how they loaded the fireworks on barges and floated them off the lakeshore, the colorful explosions competing with the beauty of the Chicago skyline. I couldn't imagine anything more spectacular.

But there would always be next year.

We were staying with Anna and Kaz. It had been a week since the terrible night in the office park. After we left Trashtown, Kaz had driven all night long and we got to their house as the sun rose high in the sky above the north side of Chicago. He'd called ahead, and Anna was waiting on the back porch for us, the dark circles under her eyes testament to her worry since we'd been gone.

A week later the dark circles had faded, and there was laughter in the house as Chub chased the cat and sang Elmo songs and Anna cooked one delicious Polish meal after another and Prairie and I slept late and we all took long walks along the lakefront. We didn't talk about what had happened. That would come soon, I was sure, as would discussions about the future—where we'd live, where I'd go to school in the fall, what Prairie would do for work. But a few things were certain: we weren't changing our names again, we weren't going to run anymore, and we were all going to stay in each other's lives somehow. Even—especially—me and Kaz.

I knew this not as a Seer knows things—I didn't know what shape our relationship would take, or where our paths would lead—but I knew he would always be there for me, just as I knew the exact shade of his eyes and the way his heartbeat felt when I leaned against his chest.

This morning Prairie announced that we had a special mission to take care of. From the looks she and Anna exchanged, I knew they'd already talked about it, but it wasn't until Prairie and I were in the car that she told me anything more. Anna and Kaz stayed behind with Chub, but Anna gave Prairie a small plastic bag as we left. Prairie slipped it into her purse, but not until I'd glimpsed the syringe it held.

"You remember Vincent," Prairie said softly as we drove northwest through the city neighborhoods.

How could I forget? I remembered his vacant staring eyes; his wasted body, motionless in the hospital bed; his waxy skin and shrunken form, kept alive only by the extraordinary efforts of experimental medicine. But most of all, I remembered the anguish in Prairie's eyes when she looked at him, even after so many years had passed since her greatest mistake.

The first time I saw Vincent, I was horrified by Prairie's choice: she had brought Vincent back from death, healed him after the last breath left his body. It was the one thing I knew must never be done, and I'd been sure I would never be tempted. But that was before I fell in love.

As we drove through the night, I thought about Kaz lying wounded in the dirt after the Pollitt house blew up. I remembered my terror when his eyes rolled up in his head, my desperate grief when I couldn't find his pulse. I remembered my tears falling on his beautiful face and the warmth of his hand in mine and I wondered if I would have had the strength to let him go.

When we arrived at the tidy brick convalescent home, Prairie chose a parking space at the far end of the parking lot, out of the glare of the streetlamps. She cut the engine and turned to me.

"This is risky," she said. "You don't have to come."

"I'm coming."

"I thought you'd say that."

She hesitated a moment longer and then she brushed her hand across my cheek, a simple gesture that made my heart tighten. I loved her so much; I didn't know how to put it into words, but I would never take her for granted again. If there was any way I could be there for her, I would never let her face another difficult moment by herself. Not only had she risked her own safety for me over and over . . . but she and I had both had enough of being alone in the world. Neither of us had parents. Neither of us had siblings. But we had each other.

When we entered the lobby, Prairie held her head high and pasted on her fake friendly smile. If I hadn't known her so well, I would have thought she was just another pretty career woman, her face obscured by the sweep of glossy hair that fell over one eye.

At the desk she paused to sign the guest register.

"I don't think we've met," she said to the attendant, a bored-looking young woman with her finger marking her page in a book. "I'm Veronica. Here visiting my dad."

"I'm just a temp," the attendant said, stifling a yawn. "Everyone wanted off for the holiday."

"Lucky them," Prairie murmured as we walked away.

At Vincent's door she quickly looked up and down the hall and then we slipped inside, and it was just as I'd remembered.

Vincent must have been handsome at one time. I'd tried imagining him the way Prairie described him—the football star, full of life, dancing with her at the high school prom. Vowing to be with her forever. Driving to the lake the night before he planned to buy her a promise ring.

The accident.

He wasn't handsome anymore. The extraordinary efforts of the researchers had seen to that, preserving his tissues long after they should have crumbled to dust. At his bedside Prairie stiffened and made a small sound—a single choked sob—and then she put her hand on my arm and gently but firmly pushed me away.

"This will only take a minute," she said, and her voice was steady.

I retreated to the corner of the room. The single lamp created shadows across the scene before me, but I saw Prairie take the small bag from her purse, prepare the syringe and slip the needle into the skin between his fingers.

He didn't react. I didn't know if it should have hurt; it didn't matter. Moments passed, Prairie's shoulders stiff and unmoving. The thing that had once been Vincent did not move; its eyes did not blink.

At last Prairie turned away from the bed, and I saw that tears streaked her smooth face.

"It's done," she said softly, and we left the room for the last time.

Back at the house she and Anna had a quick whispered conversation and then Anna hugged her. I didn't know what had been in the syringe; I did know that Anna, with her nursing school training and access to the hospital pharmacy, must have given her something deadly and hard to detect. Not that I was worried; I was pretty sure that no one would question the death of a nursing home patient whose very existence was still a mystery to researchers after all these years.

Kaz came into the kitchen carrying Chub upside down. Chub was giggling so hard his cheeks had turned bright pink. Anna took the plastic off a platter sitting on the kitchen table and I saw that she had made almond *rogaliki,* my favorite, and decorated them with red, white and blue piped icing.

"And I have a treat," she said, her eyes dancing with excitement.

She ushered us out into the backyard and took a long, narrow box from her apron. Sparklers. I'd never held one before. Each of us—me, Prairie and Chub, his hand firmly enclosed in Kaz's large one—held a sparkler to the lighter Anna produced from another pocket, and I gasped when the long wands burst into magnificent showers of dancing light. We laughed as the tiny pinpricks of heat bounced off our skin, and we trailed our sparklers through the night, writing our names in the air and making giant swirls and spirals.

At last, the final sparkler fizzled out and we were left in the dark once again. But there was a bright moon above us, and I could see Kaz's smile, the one he saved just for me. Far in the distance I heard the echoing boom of fireworks, but when Kaz wrapped his arms around me, all I heard was his heart beating, strong and sure.

Much later, I was the only one still awake in the little house. I was sharing a room with Chub, listening to him sigh and murmur in his dreams while I stared out the window at the same silvery moon.

I didn't know the future. I didn't know who I would be tomorrow, but I had made peace with who I had been until now. I couldn't change the past that had brought me this far, but I knew where I was now, in this moment. I was with people who loved me, other Banished who had made the long journey over time and distance and bloodshed and battle and loss. I was safe, loved and cherished. And it was enough.

ABOUT THE AUTHOR

Sophie Littlefield also writes crime fiction and urban fantasy for adults. Her first novel about Hailey Tarbell, *Banished,* is available from Delacorte Press. She lives with her family in Northern California. Visit her online at sophielittlefield.com.